AN INFINITE NUMBER OF

PARALLEL UNIVERSES

*In real life, you need
real friends.*

RANDY RIBAY

MeritPress | fw

Published by
Merit Press
an imprint of F+W Media, Inc.
10151 Carver Road, Suite 200
Blue Ash, OH 45242. U.S.A.
www.meritpressbooks.com

ISBN 10: 1-4405-8814-7
ISBN 13: 978-1-4405-8814-3
eISBN 10: 1-4405-8815-5
eISBN 13: 978-1-4405-8815-0

Printed in the United States of America.

10 9 8 7 6 5 4 3 2 1

Library of Congress Cataloging-in-Publication Data

Ribay, Randy.
  An infinite number of parallel universes / Randy Ribay.
    pages cm
  ISBN 978-1-4405-8814-3 (hc) -- ISBN 1-4405-8814-7 (hc) -- ISBN 978-1-4405-8815-0
(ebook) -- ISBN 1-4405-8815-5 (ebook)
[1. Friendship--Fiction. 2. Divorce--Fiction. 3. Birthmothers--Fiction. 4. Coming out
(Sexual orientation)--Fiction. 5. Automobile travel--Fiction.] I. Title.
  PZ7.1.R5In 2015
  [Fic]--dc23
                    2015012374

Cover design by Frank Rivera.
Cover and interior images © Clipart.com.

This book is available at quantity discounts for bulk purchases.
For information, please call 1-800-289-0963.

To Kathryn.
And to those who've found friendship on the
fringes, to those still searching.

Acknowledgments

Infinite thanks to: My students, for making me want to write something they might want to read; My teachers, for helping me learn to do things good; Kendall Miller and the poets at The Sieve and the Sand, for helping me to stop worrying about quality and just write; Joanna Klink, for teaching me how to make a curtain move; Explosions in the Sky, Devotchka, Sigur Rós, Youth Lagoon, Brandi Carlile, Kishi Bashi, and That Dream Was Our Life, for making music that fills my head with imagery; Coffee, for giving me superpowers; Cole, Val, Jason, Eric, Vlad, and Casey, for helping me "research" by starting a D&D campaign (goblin armor!); James, for letting me steal his car fire; Those who read early drafts of this story, for providing valuable feedback and encouragement; Aaron Kim, for being my CP (until his baby became more important than me); The South Jersey Writers Group, for being my local writer friends; Mindy McGinnis, for giving me sage advice when everything became real; The Fearless Fifteeners, for their commiseration and companionship; My therapist, Lori Lorraine, for helping me sort through all the feels; My Boys' Latin family, for being awesome; Jacquelyn Mitchard, Deb Stetson, Meredith O'Hayre, and the rest of the team at Merit Press, for believing in this story and helping to refine it; The crew at Dee Mura Literary, for helping me navigate the publishing world; My agent, Kaylee Davis, for her amazing editorial eye and for fielding my innumerable distraught texts and e-mails (fear not, there will be more!); My dog-children, for being soft and loving without fail; My family, for making sure I survived into adulthood and for putting books in our house; My wife, Kathryn, for unending support and honest feedback that sometimes makes me so sad but always makes my writing better (better writing > sadness).

Nobody can hear the music over the rustling of the plastic that covers the broken window. It flaps and billows as the air rushes past at seventy miles an hour, testing the strength of the duct tape.

Sam lowers his book and reaches between the front seats to turn up the volume, but Mari smacks his hand away without taking her eyes off the road.

Sam leans back. "That's the third time you've hit me today."

"That's the third time you've deserved it," Mari says. "I'm driving. I control the music."

"It's true. It's like a law, or something," Archie says. He removes his glasses and cleans them with his shirt. But that does not fix the cracked lens.

"Oh, so *now* you want to take my side," she says.

"What, you want me to say he's right, then?"

"This isn't about the music, Arch, and you know it."

"Then what is it about? Last night? Or what I said to Dante?"

From the front seat, Dante holds up a hand, his forearm wrapped in gauze that has bled through in spots. "Can we please not do this right now?" he asks. "Let's just get there and then go home so we don't miss too much school."

Mari adjusts the visor to shield her eyes from the sun, which hangs low in the sky above the road. Archie turns to the window to watch the farmland roll by. Sam reaches into his pocket for his phone only to remember that it's lost in the tall grass, hundreds of miles back.

The road runs straight for a stretch, hemmed by a low wooden fence. The road then curves to the left and swings to the right before straightening out again. They pass a hill where four cows gather within the shade of a few small trees next to a pond.

The road climbs. As it crests, Archie, Sam, Dante, and Mari catch their first glimpse of the mountains. They loom on the horizon, faint but formidable. It seems they are guarding the continent from itself.

Inside the car, nobody speaks.

The plastic rustles.

The radio plays.

But nobody hears it.

Archie

The Irrationality of Pi

FRIDAY

Archie stands on an uneven sidewalk examining his father's "new" place, an old three-story row house. Chipped bricks. Peeling paint. Warped wood. He removes his glasses and cleans the lenses with his shirt. It's a bright day, the kind of day for seeing things clearly.

"It looks like shit," Archie says. "No offense."

His father laughs. "You have to see what it's going to be, not what it is, Arch."

"It's going to be condemned."

"It's going to be your new home starting one week from tomorrow." His father climbs to the top of the stoop and then turns to Archie. "I'll admit the outside looks kind of rough, but we'll work on that."

"You don't know anything about this kind of stuff," Archie says.

"I'm learning," his father says, adjusting his trendy new glasses. "A friend of mine has volunteered to help. He flips houses for a living."

Archie wonders who this friend might be. His father never used to have friends. He never used to restore old homes or wear trendy eyeglasses. Archie considers pointing this out. Instead he asks, "So this is really happening?"

The approach of an electric hum makes Archie turn. He spots an old woman whirring down the middle of the street in a motorized wheelchair with a pumpkin in her lap. Archie waves. The old woman nods but does not stop.

"Trust me, it'll be gorgeous," his father says. "This neighborhood's right on the verge of turning around. There's a farmers' market. Art galleries. Great restaurants. There's even a hip bowling alley that opened up just around the corner."

"I would argue a bowling alley is, by definition, not hip."

"I guess you'll just have to see for yourself."

Archie sighs and lifts his eyes back to the house. It is balance and order that bring Archie comfort. Not this. This bothers him as much as the irrationality of pi. Even though the move is only a thirty-minute transposition, it means starting senior year at a brand new school in about a week and a half. Apart from Sam and Sarah. From Dante.

From Mari.

In one week, they'll be four points on the other side of the y-axis.

"You're absolutely certain there's no way I can just keep on living with Mom?" Archie asks. "I'll give you all my Star Wars figures. Even the Luke Skywalker with double telescoping lightsaber."

His father sighs. He walks down the front steps, puts a hand on Archie's shoulder, and squeezes—in what Archie supposes is a gesture of paternal reassurance. "As tempting as that is, you know this has already been settled. Now, come on. Check out the inside."

His father heads into the house, but Archie hangs back for a moment. He looks up. A tangle of wires chokes his view of the sky. A pair of white and red sneakers with the laces tied together is draped over one of the lines.

A stray dog approaches, tongue lolling out to one side. It reminds him of Mari's dog but mangier. Archie keeps his distance and makes his way into the house. He closes the door and locks it.

"You've already checked about my grades, right?" Archie asks, stepping into the foyer. Sunlight spills in through curtainless windows. Everything smells of cleaning product and sawdust.

"For the millionth time, yes. They will transfer exactly as they are on your transcript, and you'll be ranked accordingly. No penalty." His father spreads his arms, palms outturned. "So what do you think? Way nicer than the outside, right?"

Before answering, Archie wanders around the first floor. He stomps his foot upon the dark wood floors to check for weak spots. He pushes against an old column to test its structural integrity. He knocks on the walls because he's seen people do that in movies.

"Meh," he says, concluding his inspection.

"You have to admit it's better than the apartment. Those thin walls. The curry-scented hallways. The raccoons." He shudders.

But Archie does not want to concede anything, having conceded so much already. Granted, his father had agreed to buy him a used car after he got his license, so he'd be able to zip back over the bridge for Monday night D&D and Wednesday night Magic with his friends. But still. It wouldn't be the same as seeing them at school every day. As being able to bike a few blocks to hang out with them whenever he wanted.

And the thought of trying to find a place within the already-established social arrangement of his new school filled him with exhaustion and despair. It had taken him years to locate like-minded individuals. What would be the odds of re-creating such a miracle within just a few months? Archie could have calculated them but chose not to. Too depressing.

"Want to see your room?" his father asks, adjusting those trendy glasses again.

Archie scratches the back of his head. "Not really."

The World Quantifiable

SATURDAY

Back in his father's apartment, where the scent of curry seeps through the thin walls from the hallway and the raccoons scheme outside in the darkness, Archie lies on his bed. He stares at the tiny stalactites on the spackled ceiling, seeking patterns in vain. He curses the fact that it is not yet Monday and sits up.

He digs his laptop out of his bag, pulls it onto his lap, and powers it on.

Neither Sam nor Dante are online. But Mari is.

Archie clicks her name. He types a message but deletes it. He types another message but deletes it as well.

He doesn't know what to say, only that he wants to say something.

He sets the computer aside, stands, stretches, and walks over to the only window in his room. It offers a less than stimulating view of the parking lot. He stares at the motionless cars reflecting the sickly orange light of the building's security lamp.

Two more days.

He sighs and returns to the bed, sitting up with his back pressed against the wall. He pulls his laptop back onto his lap.

He stares at Mari's name in his list of online contacts. He wonders what she's doing right now. He wonders what she's wearing.

Shaking off the pervy thought, he pulls up World of Warcraft. Oddly enough, he doesn't really feel like running around in an imaginary land completing quests. His heart's just not in it. Still, he clicks on the option to create a new character.

Usually Archie plays mages. He loves their knowledge, their mastery of the arcane. The badassery of shooting fire out of his hands. Tonight, though, he decides to create a warrior. He maxes out the height and musculature options. He gives this warrior dark skin, dark hair, dark eyes. Scars. Tattoos. He names him Évariste, after a brilliant mathematician who died at the age of twenty fighting in a duel over the woman he loved.

He plays for an hour, low-level quests, enough to become the character, to feel a bit Évaristian himself. Exiting the game, Archie clicks on Mari's name to bring up the message box.

And before he finds the rights words, the effect dissipates. He becomes painfully self-conscious of the fact that in real life he is not a seven-foot tall, muscular, dark-skinned warrior. He is Archie. Skinny, pale, awkward Archie.

He shuts his laptop and decides he will make his move later. Tomorrow. Or Monday. Definitely before he moves into his father's new house.

He places the computer back into his bag and grabs a notebook, a pencil, his graphing calculator, and his calculus book. He opens to the dog-eared page marking the section on linear approximations and tangent planes, and he positions the book on his lap.

His shoulders relax.

Here is the world, quantifiable and predictable.

Witchcraft

SUNDAY

Archie is eating sushi at the kitchen counter. It is not his favorite food by a long shot, but he will eat it because it is his mom's favorite. She stands on the opposite side of the counter, a glass of red wine in hand, her Sunday evening sacrament.

"So how was your weekend?" she asks and then takes a sip.

"You mean besides your looming, unmotherly betrayal?" he asks.

"Yes. Besides that." She sets down her glass and uses her chopsticks to steal a piece of sushi from Archie's plate.

"Meh."

A silence settles between them as she chews. Outside, an ice cream truck's jingle approaches and recedes.

"And the new place?" she asks.

"Not so new," Archie says.

"I never thought I'd see the day that man would buy a fixer-upper. When we first moved in together, the power went out. He turned to me and said, 'I'll take care of it,' real masculine-like, and then disappeared into the basement. I figure, okay, he's going to the circuit breaker."

"Makes sense. Probably a tripped fuse, right?"

She nods. "Only, he was gone for half an hour. So finally I went downstairs, worried that maybe he electrocuted himself to death. But you know what he was doing?"

Archie shakes his head.

"He was gazing at the water heater, flashlight in one hand, stroking his mustache with the other. So I put my hands on his

12

shoulders, marched him over to the circuit breaker, showed him the tripped fuse, and then flipped it. Bam. The power was restored. And you know what he said to me?"

"What?" Archie asks.

"'Witchcraft.'" She laughs more at the memory than the objective humor of his father's comment. She picks up her wine glass again. "Doesn't that sound like something you'd say, sweetie?"

Archie takes a deep breath as he drowns a piece of sushi in soy sauce. "No offense, Mom, but I'd rather not talk about Dad—unless it's about how you've decided that I shouldn't move in with him."

She crosses her arms and shoots him a look. He imagines this is the same glare she must use to break down lying witnesses in the courtroom. "We're not having this conversation again."

"I can give you a thousand reasons this is a terrible idea," he says anyway.

She sighs. "It will be good for you. For all of us. For the last year—ever since the divorce—you've been treating your dad like a complete stranger."

"He *is* a stranger," Archie says.

"He really isn't, sweetie. He may be . . . a little different than you're used to. But he's still your dad. He's still the same person." His mom pauses for a moment and then adds, "And trust me, you don't want to go off to college without working through this. You'll regret it for the rest of your life."

Archie looks down. "There's nothing to work through."

Her eyes soften. Uncrossing her arms, she tousles Archie's hair. He pretends to pull away, to dislike it. But inside it makes him feel light and warm.

"You know, I really don't get you sometimes," she says.

"Join the club," says Archie.

"I mean it."

"Me too."

"You're the most intelligent immature person I've ever known," she says. "So if you don't want to talk about your father, what do you want to talk about?"

"I don't know," he says. But he does: Mari.

He blushes just thinking of her. It does not escape his mom's notice. She watches him squirm for a moment.

"Ooh—a girl," she says, leaning her elbows onto the counter. "Who is she?"

"Nobody."

"Ha. Spill."

"Fine," Archie admits, pushing around the last grains of rice on his plate. "But she's nobody you know."

"Sure. What's she like?"

"Smart," he says, meeting her eyes. "She's a writer. Her stories—they're so good, Mom. Brilliant. I don't know how she comes up with all of it. There's like all this depth to her mind."

"Wonderful! I knew I raised you to appreciate intelligent women. What else?"

"She's beautiful," Archie says. "Not, like, conventionally pretty. I mean—she's not ugly—just—I don't know. Not like all supermodel skinny and blonde. Anyways, I think she's hot." He hates the fact he can't find the right words.

"So what's the deal? Are you two an item yet?"

Archie lets out a sarcastic laugh. He drops his eyes back to his plate. "Ha. No."

"Why not?"

He shrugs. "I don't think she knows I like her."

"So tell her."

He crosses his arms. "It's not that easy."

"Sure it is. As a man of logic, I expect you to see that."

"Maybe for some people. But not for me. Besides, I don't think she likes me like that."

"Well, you'll never know if you don't make a move. What's the worst that can happen?"

The severe awkwardness of rejection leads to the end of our gaming nights, he thinks. He does not say it, though, for fear of giving too much away. If his mom found out it was Mari, she'd probably end up sharing his secret the next time they were all in the same room. Maybe it was a requirement of the profession, but the woman was neither indirect nor shy.

They finish the rest of their meal without talking any further about his father or his crush, and then Archie clears the table. He dumps the empty containers into the garbage, ties off the trash bag, and carries it outside, trying not to visualize the rate of change in his life as a steeply sloped graph.

He focuses instead on tasting the air. It is humid and sweet but with the faintest hint of autumn. True back-to-school weather. The sunset is a swath of orange across the horizon. The ice cream truck's jingle lilts through the neighborhood. A dog barks in the distance.

Archie drops the garbage in the trashcan at the side of the house and then spots a football in the grass. The neighbor's kid must have tossed it over the fence by accident.

He walks over to it and drops down into a three-point stance. He surveys the lawn, conjuring teammates, a packed stadium, and a scoreboard. His team is down by three.

A field goal will tie the game. But he wants to win. He winks at Mari in the stands, and then glances at the coach, who signals a play that Archie shakes off.

"Hut . . . hut . . . Blue 42 . . . hike!" he calls.

Archie hikes the ball to himself and then drops back into the pocket. He scans the field for open receivers, finally locates one, and launches a wobbly spiral into the sky.

The ball disappears over the fence.

The Table Is Simply a Table

MONDAY

Finally: Dungeons & Dragons night. The grid-based map is laid out across the center of Mari's kitchen table. The players' figures stand in the exact same spots as they did at the close of last week's session. Polyhedral dice wait to be wielded like weapons. Mari is set up at the head of the table. Her tri-fold cardboard shield conceals the notes she uses to run the game from everyone else's view.

Everything is in place.

Except there are two empty chairs and two missing players: Sam and Sarah.

They had been late before—usually because of Sarah—but never this late.

Archie checks his phone to see if either has texted him back yet. Negative.

Mari jots something down in her notebook, pressing her pen into the page with more ferocity than is probably required.

Dante rises and goes to stand at the sliding glass door, turning his giant back to Archie and Mari. He crosses his arms over his broad chest and silently stares into the early evening.

Mari lets out an exasperated breath. "Where the hell are they?"

"I'm sure they'll be here soon," Archie says. "Want to play something else while we wait? Settlers of Catan? Some who's-got-wood jokes might cheer us all up." Archie knows it's one of Mari's favorite games.

Nobody answers him.

They sink back into silence. Archie picks up his mage figurine and uses it to kick over Dante's warrior. He rolls his twenty-sided die a few times. He flicks a balled up bit of paper at Mari. It lands in her hair. He laughs. She does not. She brushes it out while muttering something under her breath that sounds like it's in a different language.

"You know, just between the three of us, I don't get what he sees in her," Archie says. When nobody speaks, he continues the conversation on his own. "I mean, yeah, she's pretty and cool and all that. But I think she's kind of a terrible person. For one, even after all these years, I get the feeling she doesn't like playing this game with us. She definitely doesn't like me. Doesn't even say hi when I run into her at school. Also, she smokes. Who smokes anymore? Ugh. And you know Sam only does because of her."

"He probably just doesn't want to be alone," Dante says, still turned away from them. "But I like Sarah."

"That doesn't count. You like everyone, D," Archie says. "But personally, I think Sam needs to dump her. You ever notice that he actually smiles and laughs when she's not around? He just seems, I don't know, lighter. She's like this parasite that just sits on his shoulder, dragging him down and draining him of all happiness—don't tell him I said that." Archie checks his phone again. "Still nothing. Let's just play with the three of us."

Mari shoots him a look as if he knows nothing about anything. "We're in the middle of a story, Arch. You need to respect the narrative. We can't just have two characters suddenly disappear."

"How difficult would that be?" Archie asks. "Let's just say they were kidnapped by goblins overnight. We look around for a bit and can't find them, so we continue on our quest and hope they turn up eventually. If they don't, then too bad, it was nice knowing them. Sayonara. Bam. Problem solved."

Mari shakes her head. "You'd still die. I designed this quest for a complete adventuring party of four. With no healer and no rogue there's not a chance you two would survive."

It is clear to Archie that this is not the night to profess his feelings to Mari. Perhaps it is Sam and Sarah's no-show, or perhaps it is her time of the month. Whatever the case, he keeps his mouth shut and goes back to rolling his die. It rattles across the table over and over again. He tries to keep track of the numbers he's rolling, appreciating the dependability of probability—on a long-enough timeline, everything falls back into place.

He considers the game pieces that have transformed Mari's dining table into their shared fantasy world nearly every Monday since the sixth grade. He gets the sense they're losing this, that he is losing them. With the impending move at the end of the week and college looming at the end of the year, he is not confident that things will fall back into place.

He gazes at what he can see of Mari as she continues writing behind the shield. Her thick black curls. Smooth brown skin. The startling green eyes behind her glasses that cause hope to bloom in him like a supernova.

Infinite futures blink to life. Most involve playing games with her forever and raising brilliant and beautiful mixed-race babies.

"I'm calling it," Mari says and starts to gather her things.

"Okay," Dante says, fishing in his pocket for his car keys.

Archie sighs. He considers bringing up his frustration about moving in with his father just to stall. But nobody ever brings up anything really personal at these sessions. These nights are all about the game, not group therapy. Sometimes he feels like they know each other's fictional character better than they actually know each other.

He watches them pack up for a moment longer, hoping they'll change their minds. But they don't. He helps clear everything away until the table is simply a table again.

Before leaving, Archie tosses his die once more. He rolls a one. Critical miss.

Relaxed Fit

TUESDAY

Archie's hands freeze over the keyboard when he hears the front door open. He listens, concerned he's about to be murdered. He has so much life left to live. But he relaxes when he recognizes the sound of his mom's heels clacking across the kitchen's tile floor.

"Archie?" she calls.

"Upstairs!" he shouts. He saves the college essay he had been editing and then makes his way downstairs. He finds her at the kitchen counter in a skirt and blazer, sifting through the mail. She is pretty and powerful even when performing such a mundane task. He fears she will start dating again soon.

"Hey," she says, dropping the pile of mail onto the counter and looking up at him.

He hugs her. She smells nice. He'll miss that.

"You're home early," he says.

"Snuck out so we could hang out together." She slips off her red heels and places them on the counter next to the pile of mail. "So what do you want to do? Movie marathon?"

"Actually," Archie says as he opens the fridge and grabs two cans of soda. He hands her one. "What if we went to the mall? You know, school starts in a week . . ."

She gives him the side eye. "Really? You, Archibald James Walker, want to go shopping? At the mall?"

His can of soda hisses as he opens it. "Yes."

Realization dawns on his mom's face. She smirks and makes her way around the counter to poke him in the heart. "The girl. You want to look hot for her."

Archie tries to brush her hand away. "No, that's not why."

"Then tell me why."

"Because." He cracks a smile.

She pokes him in the heart.

"How do they fit? You need me to grab another size for you?" His mom's voice lifts over the fitting room door louder than necessary. Striking various poses in the mirror, Archie examines himself in the jet-black, skinny-leg jeans that all the kids are wearing these days. Unfortunately, they make him look like a giraffe in black yoga pants. He turns and turns, but it's giraffe from every angle.

"Uh, maybe the same size, different style? Maybe relaxed fit," he says.

"Okay. Be right back!"

Archie steps out of the pants and folds them. While waiting for his mom to return, he flips through the T-shirts he picked up. Most of them are simple graphic tees with logos from the various games and fantasy series he knows Mari likes.

Satisfied with his selections, he steps back and examines himself in the mirror. There he is, standing in his boxers. That special sadness of self-pity washes over him. He knows he's not the ugliest kid in the world, but he's disappointed that his summer routine of pushups and protein shakes had not resulted in the bulging muscles he'd expected. If only leveling up in real life were as simple as in a game. Complete a few quests. Gain some experience. Develop special abilities.

He sighs.

Suddenly, the changing room door bursts open.

"What about these?" his mom asks, holding up a pair of jeans. Behind her, angled mirrors reflect into the store where Archie sees shoppers flipping through racks of clothes.

"Mom!" Archie pushes his mom backwards, slams the door, and locks it.

"It's just your body," she says. "Be proud of it."

Archie scrambles to put his clothes back on. "Yeah, okay. Will do."

"Well, sorry. Here are the jeans," she says, passing them over the top of the door.

"Awesome. They fit perfectly. Let's go." He emerges from the changing room, his new clothes bundled against his chest.

"I didn't get to see how they fit," his mom says.

"Like a glove."

Archie walks past her toward the registers. Thanks to back-to-school sales, the place is packed with droves of customers, mostly teenagers. They wander the store like vultures, clicking through the hangers like bones. Archie steps into the lone cash register line, which winds back on itself a couple times.

"Sure you want that pair, sweetie? The black ones seem more stylish," his mom says.

"I'm sure."

After a couple minutes, the line has not moved. Archie cranes his neck to get a better view of the delay's source. A young Hispanic girl with big hoop earrings and lips shiny with gloss stands behind the register. An ancient woman is on the other side of the counter, fishing through a change purse. She takes out three coins and places them on the counter. Just when Archie is about to celebrate her accomplishment, her shaking fingers return to the purse for more coins.

After a few moments, Archie's mom nudges him with her shoulder. "So do you not want to move in with your dad because he's gay?"

"Geez, Mom," Archie says, glancing over his shoulder. "Do you have to say it so loudly?"

"What? He *is* gay. I know this. You know this. He knows this. Granted, it took everyone a while to figure it out. The thing I still can't understand is why it's such a big deal to you, a man of science. I'd never thought you'd react like this."

Archie shifts his weight to his other foot. "Can we just talk about this later?"

"Fine. But we're going to eventually." She looks at the line, which still hasn't moved. She pulls out her credit card and hands it to Archie. "Here. I'm going to run next door. Meet me when you're done."

"Okay," Archie says, relieved to be let off the hook.

She tousles his hair and then walks away.

Not a moment later someone calls to him. "Hey, it's Skeletor!"

Archie winces at the return of his old nickname, given to him the first time he had to change clothes in front of his peers for gym class. Sure enough, he turns around to find a group of four guys from school. The "cool" kids. He forces a smile, wondering if they overhead his mom.

Archie decides to play it cool. "What's up?"

The guy who called out to Archie offers his fist for a bump. Archie considers the gesture as if it's both disgusting and amusing, perhaps amusing in its disgustingness, like a two-headed kitten. Archie frees a hand by shifting all of his purchases to one arm and then bumps the guy's fist.

The others snicker.

The first guy looks around, grinning. "Is your mom coming back? She's kind of hot."

"Yeah," says one of the other guys. "I'd hit that."

Archie feels his face reddening. If he were Évariste—or even Dante—he might be able to do something. But he's not. He's just Archie. "No," he says. "She's not."

"Damn. I'll catch up with her later," the first guy says. "Hey—you, like, know a lot about science, right?"

Archie nods.

"Awesome, 'cause I have a science question for you. Genetics, to be exact."

Archie blinks slowly, trying to wish them away. But they remain, waiting for his answer. "Okay."

The guy smirks at his friends. "So a child gets, like, half its DNA from its mom, and, like, half from its dad, right?"

"Yes." Archie clenches the new clothes to his chest. His heart rate increases.

The guy smiles. "Here's my question, bro: since your dad is gay and your mom is straight, does that mean you're, like, half gay? Like, you like blowing dudes but you don't take it up the ass? Or are you just full gay too?"

Archie does not know what to say, so he says nothing. He does nothing.

A few of the other customers in line turn to look at him.

The four guys burst with laughter. Thankfully, they don't stick around for his answer. Archie watches them leave the store, still cracking up as they merge with the endless stream of mall shoppers.

Archie glances at the register. The same old lady is still paying. She drops some coins. With glacial speed, she stoops to retrieve them. Archie looks around for a nearby hanger so that he can stab himself in the eye.

Instead, he waits a few more moments and then steps out of line. He drops his clothes in a heap on top of a random shelf and walks out.

The Ephemeral Existence of Squirrels

WEDNESDAY

B-O-O-B.

Archie smiles at the floating letters he's managed to save until the end of his bowl of cereal. Their tiny oat forms start to drift apart in the milk, so he nudges them back into place with his spoon. Hesitant to consume his creation, Archie snaps a picture with his phone, sends it to Dante. He then finishes his breakfast.

A couple of minutes pass. There's no reply. This strikes Archie as strange. He could always count on Dante to humor him even when he makes lame jokes.

Archie puts his phone in his pocket and carries his bowl to the sink. A moment later, his cell vibrates. Expecting a message from Dante, he's surprised to see that it's his father calling. He lets it go to voicemail and feels relieved when the phone stops buzzing.

Archie pours the milk into the sink, turns on the faucet, and watches the white bleed into the water as it spirals into the drain. His mind starts to drift, but then his phone starts vibrating again. His father.

Archie hesitates and then answers in case it's an emergency. "Yeah?"

"Hey, Arch, it's Dad," his father says. Archie figures he's on speakerphone because his dad's voice sounds distant and tinny. "How's it going?"

"Same ol', same ol'." There's an awkward pause where Archie expects his father to state the nature of the emergency that caused him to call twice in a row. His dad says nothing, so Archie asks, "What's up? Something wrong?"

"Listen, Arch, your mom told me—"

"Now's not a good time, father of mine. I'm really busy. Studying and stuff." Archie gazes out the kitchen window and spots two squirrels darting across the lawn, one in hot pursuit of the other. They dash up a tree and spiral around its patchy trunk, scurrying in fits and starts until finally disappearing into the leafy branches. The ephemeral existence of the squirrels leaves Archie wondering whether the one ever caught the other and what might happen if it did. What might happen if it didn't.

"Studying?" his father says, laughing. "You can't be serious. School hasn't even started yet."

"I'm getting a head start."

"You really do take after your mom."

Archie nods as though his father can see him.

A silence settles between them, the soft crackling of the speakerphone filling the space.

Finally, his father ventures into the void. "You know, Arch, I know you're upset about all this. I'd like to talk about it. And some other things. Want to grab some coffee tonight?"

Archie scratches his upper thigh through the fabric of his sweatpants. "Not really."

His father ignores the comment. "Come on, Arch. We need to clear the air."

"The air's fine. Perfect, really. Not too humid, not too dry. Low allergen factor."

"Arch . . ." his father pleads.

"I'll see you Saturday. Then we can talk all you want, forever and ever. Promise."

His father sighs. "Fine. Saturday it is."

The resigned tone in his father's voice makes Archie feel guilty. But not that guilty.

"Can't wait," Archie confirms.

"Enjoy your final days of freedom," his dad says.

Archie ends the call. He continues staring out the window. Where did those squirrels go?

A moment later his phone buzzes with a text. He's about to throw it across the room, thinking it's his father bugging him again. But his heart lightens when he sees the message is actually from Mari.

But then he reads it: *need to cancel Magic tonight. Sorry.*

it's cool. i've got a lot to do tonight, Archie shoots back. He's about to slide his phone back into his pocket but doesn't. Instead, he takes a deep breath and types another message: *hey, want to hang out tomorrow . . . just the two of us . . . ?*

He sends the message and stares at the screen, his heart beating out of his chest. But no reply appears. A few minutes later, still nothing.

His heart rate slows to normal. He sighs and lifts his eyes to the window. He watches a squirrel barrel down the tree's trunk and race away.

The second squirrel never descends.

The Complete Destruction of Humanity

THURSDAY

Archie is drenched. The sky had opened up the moment he stepped out of his house and hasn't let up since. His umbrella is little help in this windy flash flood, which has made small rivers of the sidewalks and streets. His shoes and socks are soaked through, and he can barely see thanks to the humidity that fogs the lenses of his glasses.

Yet, he is smiling. He cannot stop. It is a smile immune to the elements. Perpetual and waterproof. Constant and luminous.

It had taken over a day, but Mari had finally replied to his text: *can you come over right now?*

He had immediately answered in the affirmative and followed up with a joke, which, in retrospect, might not have been Mari's speed. But oh well. She hadn't retracted her offer.

So that is why it does not bother him when a gale-force wind turns his umbrella inside out and then plucks it from his hand. He watches as it sails away, claimed by the universe. He continues smiling.

Nothing can stop Archie right now.

Before long, he arrives at Mari's house. He steps out of the rain and onto the covered front porch. He wrings as much water as he can from his shirt and then shakes himself like a dog. It does not help much.

He examines the entryway and notices that the red front door is preceded by a glass entry door. He wonders if he should knock on the inner door or the outer door and decides on the inner door so she can hear it better but changes his mind when he realizes he'd have to open the outer door first and what if a neighbor thinks he's breaking in so he tries to remember what they usually do when he goes there for D&D.

The inner door swings open and Mari peers at him through the glass of the outer door. She's wearing a hoodie and pajama pants. Her dog, a brown lab, is at her knees. Mari pushes the outer door open. "What are you doing just standing there? You look like a creepster."

Archie runs a hand through his wet hair. "Oh. I didn't, uh, know how to knock."

"You could have rung the doorbell."

"Heh. Oh, yeah." Archie pokes the button. The bell chimes behind Mari. He smiles. She appears to be unentertained. He notices that, behind her glasses, her eyes are rimmed red like she's been crying. He wonders if he should say something but doesn't. The moment passes.

She pushes the door open all the way. Archie steps inside, dripping water everywhere. The dog begins lapping up the small puddles. "Sorry."

Mari hands him a fluffy blue towel.

"Thanks," he says and begins patting himself dry.

"Your clothes are soaked," she says. "Be right back." She disappears for a few seconds and returns with a folded pair of jeans and a shirt. She hands them to Archie. "My dad's."

"Thanks," he says and slips into the bathroom. He presses the clothes to his nose. They smell of laundry detergent.

He peels off his drenched clothes and balls them up. He stands there naked. In Mari's house. With her on the other side of the door. He takes a deep breath.

Then he realizes that there's no underwear in the clothes she brought him. Granted, it would be weird wearing her dad's underwear. But now he'll have to go commando in the pants.

Out of options, he puts on the jeans. It feels weird. He puts on the shirt, and it feels a little less weird. Examining himself in the mirror, he appears more awkward than usual thanks to the ill-fitting clothes. But nothing can stop Archie.

He steps out of the bathroom, smiling.

Mari folds her arms over her chest. "Just to be clear, I'm not going to have sex with you. Here, give me your wet clothes so I can throw them in the dryer."

The comment catches Archie off guard, but he recovers. "Obviously," he says, looking down at himself, "you can't afford this."

"Seriously, though, I just needed to hang out with someone."

"Everything okay?" he finally asks.

Mari shrugs. She pulls the sleeves of her hoodie down over her hands. "I'd rather not talk about it. Let's just watch something."

"You're the boss."

Archie follows her down the hallway. He catches himself looking at her butt, so he shifts his gaze to the pictures on the walls. They've been there forever, but Archie doesn't remember ever looking at them. Most are school photos taken of Mari and her brothers, arranged in such a way that the subjects age in a linear progression. There are a few posed, professional shots of the entire family. In most they're all wearing matching outfits. Archie knows Mari was adopted, yet he's struck by how white the rest of her family is. They appear happy enough, but Mari's brown skin stands out. He wonders if any of it ever bothers her.

They enter the living room. Mari pops a disc into the DVD player while Archie sits down on the short side of the L-shaped sofa. Uninterested, the dog trots away and lies down with a huff on its bed in the corner. The rain picks up, thrumming upon the roof.

Mari turns on the television. A familiar theme song suddenly blasts through the surround sound.

"*Firefly,*" he says. "I approve."

Mari turns to Archie and says something, but he can't hear her. *What?* he mouths.

She turns down the volume and repeats her question. "You want something to eat or drink? Like popcorn?"

"Why would I want to drink popcorn?"

She looks at him, unamused.

"Tough crowd," Archie says.

"You know what I mean. Would you like something to eat—such as popcorn—and slash or, would you like something to drink—such as not popcorn?"

"Sure," he says. "Popcorn sounds good. What kind of non-popcorn beverages do you have?"

"The usual."

"All right, I'll take the purple stuff."

Mari rolls her eyes and heads into the kitchen.

Archie stares at the menu screen and hums along with the theme music as he waits. Behind him, he hears Mari open and close a cabinet, and then rip open plastic packaging. The microwave door pops open and then slams shut, buttons beep, and then there's the steady hum of shooting particles. He takes a moment to appreciate the science behind that particular innovation, recalling when he had read somewhere that people used to call it a "science oven" back when it was first invented.

Archie drums his fingers on his knees. He looks down at his lap. The crotch region of the jeans are bunched up in such a way that he fears it looks like he has a boner, so he flattens it out. Just to be sure, he picks up a throw pillow and uses it to cover his lap.

He turns around to check on the snack progress and sees Mari bent over. She is looking for something at the back of the bottom shelf of the refrigerator. It is a beautiful sight. Like two integrals ready to be solved. As he continues to watch, the popcorn kernels in the microwave start popping faster and faster. Just when it seems like they're going to explode, the microwave sounds a long beep and Mari straightens up. Archie turns back to the TV. He clears his throat and readjusts the pillow in his lap.

A few moments later, Mari returns to the living room carrying a glass of soda in each hand and a bowl of popcorn between her forearms. "Thanks for your help."

"You're welcome," Archie says.

Mari takes a seat at the opposite end of the couch from Archie and draws her legs up underneath her. She picks up the remote and presses play. "I guess chivalry really is dead."

"I thought you were a modern woman," Archie says.

When the episode ends, Archie and Mari can't stop talking about how great the show is and how much of a loss to the world it was when the network cancelled it before the conclusion of its first season.

Once they exhaust their conversation about the episode, Mari excuses herself. When she returns a few minutes later, she sits down just a couple feet away from Archie.

"So," he says, checking his watch.

Mari props her left elbow on the top of the couch and leans her head against the palm of her hand. She smiles. "Want to watch another episode?"

Archie picks up the throw pillow and hugs it to his chest. "There's nothing more I'd rather do. In fact," he says, turning to her and putting on a mock evil face, "I would kill my own mother to continue watching this show with you."

Mari's smile disappears. She puts down the remote. She covers her face with her hands and leans forward, resting her elbows on her knees.

She starts sobbing. It is sudden and terrible.

Having never been confronted with a crying girl, Archie does not know what to do. He looks upon her as he might a newly arrived alien: perplexed by its strangeness and apprehensive of its potential to lead to the complete destruction of humanity.

According to the movies and TV he'd seen, he should move next to her, place an arm over her shoulders, and say something reassuring. Yet he doesn't dare touch her for fear of doing it incorrectly, and he doesn't say anything for fear of saying the wrong thing.

She continues sobbing into her hands.

"On second thought, it's getting kind of late," he says.

She nods, face still hidden behind her hands.

"I'll let myself out," he says, rising.

Archie stands there for a moment longer, replaying what he said. He does the math.

It doesn't add up.

"I'm sorry," he says and then walks out, forgetting his clothes in the dryer.

He steps back into the rain, smiling no longer.

Mari

Cold Beyond Comprehension

FRIDAY

Mari sets her pen to the page, her head full of stories. She manages to write a couple paragraphs, but then the chattering Spanish from the waiting room's television colonizes her mind. After cursing herself for forgetting her headphones, Mari closes her notebook. She looks up at the screen.

There is a man sitting with a woman. Both look groomed yet unkempt, proud yet ridiculous. The host asks them a question; they respond. The crowd boos. The camera keeps cutting to a second man, standing backstage, pacing like a caged animal. When the second man finally decides to walk on to the stage, he rushes toward the first man, anger blazing in his eyes. The first man rises to meet him. Security guards materialize out of thin air and restrain the men. The camera keeps cutting between shots of the scuffle, the guffawing audience, and the eternally smirking and shrugging host.

Even though there are no subtitles, Mari can guess what is happening. The two men are probably brothers or best friends. The woman, originally one man's lover, now probably carries the child of the other.

Mari can't even begin to comprehend how people get into such situations—and then want to resolve it on national television. She wonders if the guests, the host, and the audience are even real. If they are, she wonders what the hell is wrong with them, why they feed off one another's pain like parasites.

"Can I turn this off?" Mari finally asks the receptionist.

The receptionist glances around the waiting room. She picks up the remote and hits the mute button.

"Thanks," Mari says, though her eyes linger on the now pantomimed drama.

After summoning the power to look away, Mari opens her notebook and rereads what she had written, trying to regain her flow.

But she can't. It's gone. She can't find whatever words or sentences or ideas she meant to set down next. It is like walking into a room to retrieve something only to forget what it was she had wanted.

Mari sighs. Closes her notebook.

She leans back. A potted plant sits in the corner of the room. Mari cannot tell if it is real or fake. She scans its leaves for imperfections, always reliable evidence of authenticity, and then reaches over and takes one between her fingers. She concludes that it is fake.

She pushes around the magazines. None of them interest her, but one cover catches her attention. It features a girl riding on her mother's back, enjoying a day at the beach. This reminds Mari of when she was little and her mom used to take her out on "Ladies' Night" every Tuesday night. Usually, they would dress up and start with dinner at a nice restaurant. After dinner, her mom would have some surprise activity planned for them. Sometimes they'd see a movie that her brothers and dad would never be caught dead watching. Sometimes they'd go to the mall. Sometimes they'd paint pottery.

Most of it had been girlie stuff like that. Stuff her mom loved and Mari wished she loved more. But occasionally they'd go to the bookstore and Mari would be allowed to select any one book she wanted to buy. Sometimes they'd drive to one of the local colleges for a poetry reading. Or maybe they'd catch an old fantasy movie playing downtown. Stuff Mari enjoyed.

Once, they travelled to the shore even though it was an hour away, and even though it was the middle of winter. Mari was twelve. She remembers the Atlantic crashing into forever, cold beyond comprehension. And snow blanketed the beach—it glowed so that in the darkness they didn't even need flashlights. Each step pressed a fresh footprint into that bright, bright snow. When Mari's feet got too cold, her mom let her ride piggyback as they returned to the car.

But it has been years since the last Ladies' Night, all because of Mari.

The puzzled looks people gave them. The questions they asked. All because Mari and her adoptive mother did not match every-one's idea of mother and daughter. Their skin, their hair, their features—too different for the world to make sense of them. It had just become too much for her. So Mari had lied and told her mom she was getting too old for their weekly hangout.

Mari glances at a clock on the wall and finds that almost an hour has passed. She sighs, even though it's not like she has any Friday night plans.

The main doors into the waiting room suddenly slide open. A wrinkled old man, hunched over a walker, inches across the threshold. A tuft of white hair clings to one side of his bald, liver-spotted head. The receptionist greets him by name and tells him not to worry about signing in.

The man nods and then slowly makes his way toward the seats, approaching the row opposite of Mari. Once he arrives—Mari had serious concerns he might keel over at any given moment—he turns and carefully lowers himself into a chair as if he were trying to dock a spaceship with the International Space Station. The seat's foam cushion sighs as he finally lands. He then closes his eyes and either falls asleep or dies.

Mari looks back up at the television to watch the people argue. She considers asking the receptionist to unmute it, but that would be too embarrassing.

She looks back at the man. He has not moved. Mari begins to fear that he may have actually died. But then he lets out a prolonged fart. It starts out as a low rumble, picks up momentum, and then peters out in a few gradual toots. And just as the last of the gas seems to escape, there's one final, definitive blast. Almost like a sneeze.

But the man still sits with his eyes closed, showing neither motion nor shame.

Mari almost begins to laugh at the absurdity of the moment until the stench hits her. It is thick and pungent. She pulls the collar of her T-shirt over her nose.

Just then the door leading back to the exam rooms swings open and Mari's mom emerges. She smiles at Mari and gestures for her to wait a moment. After a brief conversation with the receptionist, she returns to Mari.

"Can we go now?" Mari asks, voice muffled by her shirt.

"We sure can," her mom says, smiling at Mari. But a second later she drops the smile and wrinkles her nose. Mari notices her mother catch wind of the fart and starts to laugh. Her mom tries to keep a straight face. "But remember that we have a couple more errands to run."

"I hope they're as exciting and fragrant as this one," Mari says.

On their way out to the parking lot, Mari glances back to see the receptionist move from behind her desk and water the plant in the corner.

"Your eighteenth birthday is eight months from today," Mari's mom says. She flips the turn signal, checks the rearview mirror, and changes lanes.

"I am aware," Mari says. "That's a red light."

"I am aware," her mom says, hitting the brakes. Once stopped, she examines her manicured nails.

"So . . ." Mari says.

"So . . . what?" her mom says.

"Is there a reason you brought up my birthday which is, like, a year away still?"

"Not really. Just making conversation."

"That's not conversation," Mari says. "That's just a statement. A conversation requires a back-and-forth interaction. Like this. This is a conversation. About conversation. Don't you agree?"

"Sorry," her mom says, still looking at her nails.

"Green," Mari says, tilting her chin in the direction of the light.

Her mom looks up and steps on the gas. The car jolts forward.

"Actually . . ." her mom says. "Oh, never mind."

Mari leans her head back and closes her eyes. "Geez, Mom. What?"

She glances at Mari, turns her eyes back to the road, and exhales. "I had an ulterior motive for taking you along with me today. There's something I want to tell you . . . but we're supposed to wait until you're eighteen."

"So now you have to tell me," Mari says. "You can't say something like that and then not."

"But now I'm thinking maybe I should wait . . ."

"What is it?"

"Promise me you won't tell your father I told you."

". . . Okay."

"So we adopted you when you were a baby," she says.

Mari covers her mouth with her hand in mock surprise. "Oh my!"

"You didn't let me finish," her mom says, playfully slapping Mari's arm.

"Okay, finish."

"Okay. So." Her mom takes a deep breath and then restarts. "We adopted you when you were a baby. We've always told you that if you ever had any questions about it, you could ask us. But you haven't ever."

"Because I don't care," Mari says, gazing out the window at the passing buildings.

"I know, and we've respected that. But as part of our adoption agreement, we're required to give you your biological mother's name and contact information when you turn eighteen if you haven't requested it by then."

"You have to? Like legally?"

"Yes."

"So then why tell me now?"

"In case you wanted it now."

"I don't."

"You sure?"

"Yes. And I won't want it in eight months, either."

"Well, if you change your mind—"

"I won't."

They pull into the driveway, and Mari's mom kills the engine. They sit in silence, staring at the closed garage door. Eventually, Mari reaches up and hits the button to open it. She jumps out of the car and disappears into the house.

Her Hidden Multiverse

SATURDAY

On second thought, Mari decides to destroy the world.

She crosses out the final paragraphs and brainstorms how she will do it.

It is late. A light in her room is the only one on in the entire house. Her door is closed, and an instrumental track set on repeat plays through her headphones. She lies on her stomach across the floor.

She pauses, pressing the tip of the pen to her lips, and searches the walls for inspiration.

A storm of pictures and pages surround her. Faded colors, curling corners, and thumbtack holes mark the age of each. There are postcards from cities she's visited and cities she wants to visit. There are pictures of people and animals and buildings and clouds and trees and lakes and campfires and statues and streets and cemeteries. There are posters of famous paintings enhanced with handwritten verses taken from some of her favorite lines of poems and songs. There are drawings of fantasy creatures and landscapes. There are yellowing pages removed from forgotten books bought from garage sales, the passages of which contain no particular significance to her.

There is a photo of her younger brothers at the beach. They crouch in smooth white sand while forming a castle. Their pale skin stings with sunburn. The photographer's shadow reaches for the water next to them.

On the same wall, high above her mirrorless dresser, there is a photo of her parents on their wedding day. Her dad stands behind her mom with his arms around her waist. Both stare slightly above-camera and smile blissfully with love and forever.

And opposite her dresser, there is a picture of Mari's best friend who is also adopted. She smiles at the camera, pale pink tongue lolling out to one side over white fangs and black lips. Macadamia, the nine-year-old chocolate lab mix in the photograph, now lies on the floor next to Mari. She yawns and stretches her legs, pressing her back into Mari's side.

The right ending suddenly comes to Mari. She starts scribbling into her notebook, pen lifting and dipping like flames licking at the sky.

Mari puts the period on the final sentence and then reads through the entire story. Satisfied, she tears the pages from the notebook and staples them together. She walks over to her closet and pulls out the milk crate she uses as a filing cabinet.

She breathes in old paper and ink as she thumbs through the file folders, which are labeled according to their subjects. There are folders for her D&D stories and fan fiction, and a few attempts at original fantasy and sci-fi. But the thicker folders are those labeled with the names of her family members and friends.

Among the innumerable words are such worlds in which Dante is a midget, Archie's an orphan, Sam never meets Sarah, and her brothers are girls. One folder contains the various adventures of Macadamia lost in the wild. Another holds pages wherein Mari is adopted by different families, ranging from the abusive to the loving, the affluent to the poor, the animal to the robotic.

But the thickest folder is the one labeled "Biological Mother." One of her very first stories, only a few sentences long and written in crayon, describes the woman as an exiled alien from another planet who had to abandon Mari to protect her from evil aliens.

And there are others in which she is a mortal who slept with a god. A famous artist. A drug addict. A zombie. A rape victim. A politician.

But in none of these worlds does the woman keep Mari.

This is the folder into which Mari tucks her most recent story of a world destroyed. She then slides the crate, her hidden multi-verse, back into her closet and closes the door.

She hits the light switch, joining her darkness to that of the rest of the house, and then slides beneath her covers. Macadamia hops onto the bed and cuddles next to Mari. Mari kisses her on the nose. Macadamia grumbles because she cannot purr.

Mari closes her eyes but does not fall asleep. A fire burns in the forefront of her mind, a fire that refuses to be extinguished.

These Words Are a Lighthouse

SUNDAY

Mari stares at the page like someone looking down a well after dropping a coin.

The top of her letter reads, "Dear," but she does not know what noun of address to use. *Mom? Mother? Biological Mother? Woman-I've-Never-Met? Woman-Who-Abandoned-Me-and-Probably-Doesn't-Even-Remember-Who-I-Am?*

She does not know the woman's name, and she does not have a mailing address yet. All she has to do is ask her mom. But to do so would remove the fiction, and the fiction keeps Mari safe, warding against reality. It has always been that way.

Mari chews on the end of her pen. She readjusts her headphones.

She tears the page out of the notebook, crumples it into a ball, and tosses it into the metal wastebasket. On the fresh page she starts over: "Hello."

An hour later, Mari feels like she has just finished running a marathon. Her eyes are blurry and her hand is cramped. She has written six pages, front and back. After overcoming that initial road block, her words flowed effortlessly. The letter is a testament to her curiosity, her sadness, her anger.

But she feels better having put these emotions on the page. These words are a lighthouse. A transcontinental railway. A stack of dynamite.

She folds the pages and stuffs them into an envelope. She grabs her keys and heads to the front door. Macadamia trots after her.

"I'm going out," she tells her parents, who are on the couch watching television.

"Keep an eye on the gauges," her dad says. "She's been acting funny."

"Will do."

Mari drives a few minutes away to her favorite diner, a place where she likes to go to think. She steps inside to find the place vibrating with the hum of conversation and the clanging of dishes. The scent of frying food fills the air.

As Mari waits to be seated, a middle-aged black woman walks through the door and then stands next to Mari. Mari catches herself wondering—as she has countless times before—if this woman is her real mother. It's a stupid thought, she knows, but that doesn't prevent it from occurring.

Eventually, a man walks in, puts his arm around the woman's shoulder, and leads her to the hostess booth to request a table for two. Mari lingers as they talk and laugh. Mari then takes her regular seat at the counter with the other lonely souls.

Even though it's getting late, Mari orders a cup of coffee. A moment later the waitress puts a steaming mug in front of her. Mari puts her hands around it, enjoying the warmth.

For some reason, Mari's mind wanders to a friend she had in the third grade, a Dominican girl named Clara who also wrote stories. They would often play a game together that they called "Once Upon a Time." One of them would begin a story with a single sentence and then pass the paper so that the other person could add a new sentence to the story. They would continue passing the paper back and forth, weaving a disjointed, ridiculous narrative until they were laughing so hard they were crying, on the verge of peeing their pants.

Mari used to go over to Clara's house all the time. Clara had a great mom. Warm and loving. Forever cooking and hugging. And Clara looked just like her.

But when the third grade ended, Clara and her mom moved back to the DR, and Mari went back to reading and writing by herself in corners and under trees.

Mari's mind returns to the present when a man slides onto the stool next to her. He reeks of alcohol and sadness. He has short, gray hair and purple bags under his eyes. Before Mari can ask who he is, the man says, "Excuse me, Miss. Would you like to attend the party?"

Mari hesitates. "What party?"

"The party. In my pants."

"I do not," Mari says. "Please leave."

"Well, I thank you for your time."

The man tips an imaginary hat and leaves.

Mari takes out the letter and rereads it.

Back in her room, Mari opens a window. She moves a lit candle to the sill and empties her trashcan onto the floor. She holds the corner of the envelope to the flame and watches it catch. The fire spreads quickly, devouring the paper. The words and the space between them dissolve into smoke, never to be read. The acrid scent fills her room despite the open window.

The flame and heat get dangerously close to Mari's fingers, so she drops the burning letter into the empty metal wastebasket. It's not long before everything she felt turns to ash.

All She Can Do

MONDAY

At first Mari thinks that she must have something on her face because Archie keeps gawking at her. Kind of like he wants to say something but doesn't. Whatever the reason, it's weirding her out, so she turns her attention to her notebook where she's sketching a winged minotaur that wields a flaming broadsword. It's the boss the party will encounter at the end of this quest.

If they ever get there.

"Where the hell are they?" Mari asks.

Dante continues to stand silently at the sliding glass doors for some reason. Archie starts talking, but Mari doesn't really pay attention. He's forever saying something, after all.

She hopes Sam and Sarah aren't fighting. If they break up, she's certain Sarah would stop coming to D&D night. Then Mari would have to rewrite the entire world.

But that wasn't the likely scenario. Sam and Sarah usually got along well enough most of the time—primarily because Sam just went along with whatever Sarah said. Like their characters. When they first started playing, Sam had wanted to be the rogue. With Archie calling mage and Dante claiming a warrior, that left Sarah with the cleric. She said that was boring and didn't want to play. So Sam volunteered to be the cleric, the healer, and Sarah got to be the rogue.

Mari's train of thought is interrupted when she feels something land in her hair. She looks up and peers over her shield to find Archie grinning at her. She brushes away whatever it was he threw.

"*Yag thellaru*," she curses in a fictional language she created years ago for their fantasy world. "Dumb boy."

Archie looks confused.

Mari turns back to her drawing.

Archie starts talking again. Starts ogling her again.

Then he starts rolling his twenty-sided die. Over and over and over.

She grits her teeth. She digs her pen into the page.

Mari tries to let it go because she recognizes that she's not being fair to him. Her indecision about contacting her biological mother is getting to her.

Still, it's all she can do to keep from picking up Archie's die and launching it out the window, launching *him* out the window.

"I'm calling it," Mari says and closes her notebook.

The Universe Isn't Here to Reassure Us

TUESDAY

Mari watches her blood fill the tube. The red liquid sloshes and foams as it pours in the container, the level rising past the fifteen cups mark.

"There's a lot of blood in me," Mari says.

"There's a lot of everything in you," her mom says. For some reason, she says it like she's sad even though this is the first Ladies' Night they've had in years. Her mom had surprised Mari by suggesting they do so. Mari agreed. And they got into the car and drove to the Franklin Institute.

Mari steps off the platform that has weighed her in order to calculate and then demonstrate the contents of her circulatory system. A small boy pushes past her for his turn.

"How long has it been?" Mari asks, wandering away from the exhibit.

Her mom trails behind her. "Maybe ten years? You must have been in the second or third grade last time we were here."

"Man, I'm getting old."

"You have no idea."

A few children run about, bouncing and bounding, their parents in tow. For some reason, the museum is far less crowded than usual.

Mari stops in front of the exhibit with the model heart the size of a small house. "It's smaller than I remember."

"You've grown," her mom says. "Everything looks smaller once you're bigger."

"It used to scare me when I was a kid. Felt like I was playing inside of a giant's chest. Thought I might kill him if I bumped against the sides too much." Mari turns to her mom. "Want to go inside?"

Her mom shakes her head. "I'll wait for you out here."

"Oh, come on," Mari says, pulling her mom by the hand. Her mom relents.

They slip through the narrow entrance and step into the right atrium. Strategically placed lights cast eerie shadows in the recesses of the interior. The sound of a beating heart plays through unseen speakers, and a deep and steady rhythm echoes throughout the cavernous space. It is comforting yet ominous.

Thump-THUMP . . . Thump-THUMP . . . Thump-THUMP . . .

Mari drops her mom's hand and runs her fingers along the heart's plaster walls. The pink paint has been rubbed white from hundreds of thousands of touches, people who had come before her doing the same. She makes her way through the tunnel-like main artery, ducking to avoid the low spots in the ceiling.

"Still there?" Mari asks over her shoulder.

"Always."

Thump-THUMP . . . Thump-THUMP . . . Thump-THUMP . . .

The pathway leads them up a narrow set of stairs that opens in a tiny balcony at the top of the heart. Mari pauses to survey the room from twelve feet in the air. A small group of children wearing identical bright yellow shirts squeezes past. Mari's mom smiles after them.

They proceed through the passageway and down into the next chamber. Mari stops, presses a finger against the side of the heart, and begins tracing the network of blue and red veins painted along the walls.

A small black girl, not older than five or six, walks into the room, looking around in wonder. She grasps Mari's free hand while still examining the heart's shadowy interior.

"I'm scared, Mommy," she says. She pulls Mari toward the exit.

Thump-THUMP . . . Thump-THUMP . . . Thump-THUMP . . .

Mari looks down, amused that the girl has mistaken her for her mother. She then glances up at her own mom. A shadow seems to pass over her mom's face.

"I'm sorry, honey," Mari says to the girl in a soft voice. "I'm not your mommy. But I'm sure she's her somewhere around here."

The girl lets go of Mari's hand when she realizes her mistake. A moment later, a woman appears through the main artery. The girl runs to her and they exit the left ventricle, hand-in-hand. Silence settles back into the chamber.

Thump-THUMP . . . Thump-THUMP . . . Thump-THUMP . . .

Mari is about to follow behind them when she notices that her mom has turned away. She is covering her face with her hands.

"You okay?" Mari says, coming up next to her and wrapping an arm around her shoulder.

Her mom turns and wraps her arms around Mari. When she pulls away from the embrace, Mari sees that her eyes are brimmed with tears. This scares Mari more than the possibility of killing a giant.

"What's going on, Mom?" she asks.

"Nothing. I just . . . I need to step outside for a moment. Take as long as you want."

Her mom rushes out of the heart. Mari pauses to wonder what might be wrong and then follows after her.

Emerging from the left ventricle, Mari scans the exhibit room. There's a skeleton slowly riding an elliptical machine to her right, a spiraling display of various animal hearts to her left, but no sign of her mom.

She walks back into the main atrium, past the gigantic, godlike statue of a seated Benjamin Franklin. The hall brightens and then dims as a cloud passes over the skylights.

Mari steps out of the museum and onto the top of the marble stairs that lead down to the busy street. The sound of traffic is unusually loud. She squints at the brightness of the day, shields her eyes from the sun, and spots her mom to the left of the staircase. Her mom is sitting on a low wall in front of a sculpture of an early plane's wire frame. Birds flit in and out of the iron skeleton.

"Hey." Mari sits down next to her.

"Hi," her mom says. She wipes her eyes with a crumpled tissue and then drops her hands to her lap.

They sit and watch the traffic pass, the noises weaving together in the air.

"Want to tell me what's up?" Mari asks.

"Sorry," her mom says, smiling through new tears. "I tried to not cry. But then I saw you with that little girl. And it made me think . . ." She trails off.

"About what?"

Her mom sighs. "How someday you'll have kids."

"Maybe," Mari says. "I haven't decided yet. I might just be a crazy cat lady."

Her mom laughs.

"But why'd that make you cry?" Mari asks. "Is this about me not wanting to contact my biological mother?"

Mari's mom stands. "Let's walk." She tilts her head in the direction of a large fountain on the other side of a grassy area in front of the museum.

Mari stands. Her mom loops her arm through Mari's. They cross the street and then make their way along the sidewalk, stepping beneath the dappled shadows of trees whose leaves are just beginning to turn.

They sit at one of the benches along the edge of the circular clearing and stare at the fountain that consists of three large statues, nude figures reclining and facing away from the center. Each one has an animal behind its head that spouts arcing water into the shallow pool. Even though the air carries an autumn coolness, a few kids splash around in the water.

"I think it's important for you to contact your birth mother," her mom says, picking up their conversation.

Mari's face hardens. "Why?"

Her mom hesitates. Looks up at the sky. "I have cancer."

She looks at her mom. She feels like she's fallen into the bottom of a deep well. "What?"

"I have cancer."

"No."

"Yes."

Mari turns away. She gazes into the fountain's spraying water. Everything seems louder. The fountain. The traffic. The wind in the leaves. But nothing seems real.

"I started crying back there, in the heart," her mom says, "because I thought about how I might never get to see you have children."

"Or cats," Mari adds quietly.

Her mom laughs. "I always thought you were more of a dog person."

"Are you going to die?" Mari asks after a moment.

She shrugs. "I hope not."

"What kind is it?"

She presses her hand across her left breast. "Stage three. The doctor said that I have about a seventy percent chance of survival with treatment—so that's good news. It could be a lot worse."

Mari nods, but her mind flashes to all the times she's rolled a one or a two with a six-sided die. "What kind of treatment?"

"Chemotherapy . . . and a mastectomy, most likely."

Mari tries to imagine the missing breast beneath her mom's shirt. "When did you find out?" she asks.

"The biopsy was last Friday."

Mari realizes that was when she drove her mom to the doctor's office. She remembers the muted talk show. The flatulent old man. The artificial plant that had seemed so real. She had thought nothing of it at the time, figuring it was just a routine visit.

"They called with the results the other day," her mom adds.

"Does dad know? Do Eric and Andrew?"

"Dad does. We wanted to tell you first since you're the oldest. Your father and I are going to talk to them tonight."

The world darkens as a large cloud blocks the sun. Mari looks up and notes that it will probably be a while before the sun reemerges. It might even rain.

Mari wants to cry but all she feels is anger. "I hate that this has to happen to you. You're like the nicest person in the world. Why couldn't this happen to some child molester or rapist or politician instead? Why does it have to be you?"

Her mom takes a slow, deep breath. "I've been asking myself that question a lot lately."

"And?"

"And there's no answer. It's out of my control. It just did. It happened."

"That's reassuring."

"The universe isn't here to reassure us," her mom says.

"Then why is it here?"

"That's another question I've been asking myself a lot lately."

"And?" Mari asks.

"I'll let you know when I figure it out."

Mari closes her eyes and leans forward, resting her elbows on her knees. The wind picks up, rustling the leaves and spraying the fountain's spouting water in a mist that carries to Mari and her mom. They do not notice.

"So this is why you told me about the contact information before my birthday?"

Her mom nods. "I want to be there for you. To help you work through things."

"Do you really think you'll die before then?"

"Probably not. But you never know. I don't want to take any chances anymore."

Mari is silent for a while, and then says, "I doubt she'll want to meet me."

"She does."

"How do you know?"

"We've been writing each other for years."

"And you never told me?"

"I'm sorry, Mar. It was part of the adoption agreement. I've had to provide her with annual updates, and she's been free to communicate with me. But unless you request it on your own, she can't contact you directly until you're eighteen."

"Why?" Mari asks.

"I guess they—the adoption agency—thought you'd be mature enough to handle it by then."

"Do you think I'm ready now?"

"I do."

Mari sighs. "So tell me something about her."

Mari's mom opens her purse and pulls out a white envelope. She holds it out to Mari.

"The contact information's in here. Along with a letter."

Mari takes it. She's surprised by its lightness. Probably just a single page, Mari guesses. Nothing like the epic letter she had written and promptly burned.

Her mom puts her arm around Mari, squeezes her, and kisses her on the head. "You'll never know how grateful I am to have been the one to raise you."

Mari does not know if she believes in God, but she prays. She prays for light, a light so quiet and so clear, it will sweep over the world and heal everything and everyone.

Still, though, she cannot cry.

This Will Not Turn Out Well for the Cat

WEDNESDAY

"What happens when we die?" Mari's little brother asks. He sits cross-legged on the floor, two feet from the television, holding a bowl of soggy cereal. Macadamia is lying at his side, her head resting on her paws and her eyes also on the television.

On the screen, a cartoon mouse has just used a cleaver to chop a cartoon cat into several pieces.

Mari is on the couch wearing her mom's old college T-shirt, its crest faded and cracking from a thousand washings. "I don't know," Mari says, because she doesn't. Despite giving the question a lot of thought in the last day. "People think different things."

"Like what?"

"Well, religious people think that you have a soul, kind of like a spirit inside of you that lives forever."

"Like a ghost?" her brother asks.

"I don't know. Maybe. Anyways, they think that after your body dies, your soul goes to an afterlife. If you're good, it goes to heaven. If you're bad, it goes to hell." Mari's mind flashes back to the one time she went to church with Dante years ago. She had thought it strange how the congregants held their palms to the sky and swayed while praying, as if in a trance. As if anyone could be that certain of anything.

"What if you're both?"

Mari shrugs.

"How do you know how to be good?"

Mari shrugs. "Their religion tells them, I guess."

"Then it's easy."

"Not necessarily."

"Why not?"

Mari wonders the same. She wants to play the part of the wise elder, but she feels short on wisdom. She settles on an answer. "Sometimes things get confusing."

Andrew spoons cereal into his mouth, some milk from the spoon dripping back into the bowl as he continues staring at the TV. Mouth full, he asks, "Are we religious?"

Mari shrugs. "Not really. But you can decide what to believe for yourself when you're older."

He turns to Mari. He looks at her with the same sad blue eyes of their mom, so different from the green of Mari's. "What do you think?"

Mari considers his question for a moment. "It just kind of ends."

"Like closing your eyes?"

"Maybe." Mari closes her eyes, trying to imagine it. "Except you probably won't be able to think or dream anymore."

Andrew's face scrunches as he tries to comprehend nothingness. "So when I die, it'll be like turning off the TV?"

She opens her eyes. "Maybe. Nobody knows for sure."

"That makes me sad."

Mari's afraid he's going to cry, but then he turns back to the television and continues eating his cereal. The cartoon cat has come back to life and has captured the mouse. Although the cat is strapping sticks of dynamite to the bound mouse, Mari is certain this will not turn out well for the cat.

In that moment, Mari decides to cancel Magic tonight. She sends a text out to the group, drawing her attention away from the episode's foregone conclusion.

Her phone chirps with a reply from Dante: *no problem. everything alright?*

In her reply she lies that everything is all right.

The next text is from Archie: *it's cool. i've got a lot to do tonight.*

Then her phone falls silent. Nothing from Sam. Nothing from Sarah.

A moment later, it chirps with another message from Archie: *hey, want to hang out tomorrow . . . just the two of us . . . ?*

She wonders if it is a joke.

Does he like her?

Mari doesn't know how to respond to the strange request so she just doesn't. She sets her phone down and turns her attention back to the TV. But the screen is now blank. Her brother and Macadamia have left.

Mari runs her hands along the surface of the tomato's skin as the water washes over it. Setting it aside, she cleans two more and then pulls out a cutting board.

Mari's mom is next to her, quartering raw chicken. Macadamia sniffs around their feet, scavenging for dropped food. The annoying voices of sports announcers spill over from the living room TV. Video game explosions rumble through the ceiling from her brothers' room upstairs.

Her mom brings the butcher's knife down with a heavy *thunk*.

Mari sets to dicing the tomatoes.

Her mom looks over. "Still upset about your friends cancelling another game night?"

"Of course." Mari fails to mention that she cancelled it because she doesn't know how much time she has left with her mom. Why waste it playing some pointless game with friends whose fictional characters she knows better than the people behind them?

Her mom smiles. "Well, some things are just out of your control. But it's nice to have you help me in the kitchen. Those boys of ours are useless."

Mari shrugs. "It does seem to be a trait of the gender."

Her mom finishes with the chicken, pushes it aside, and washes her hands in the sink. She begins opening cabinets and pulls out a few bottles of spices. After setting them out on the counter, she examines Mari's work.

"You didn't cut out the stems first?"

Mari continues dicing.

"I've told you to cut out the stems first before."

"You've told me a lot in my life," Mari says.

"Sometimes I'm afraid I haven't told you enough." Mari's mom sets to seasoning the chicken.

As her words hang in the air, Mari wonders if this is how it will be from now on. Every conversation ready to take a turn for the grim. Every sentence ready to foreshadow. Her mom must sense it too because she changes the subject. "So. School starts in a week. Excited?"

"About as excited as that chicken you're butchering."

"Oh, please. I bet you are. I mean, it's your *senior* year."

"It's just school, Mom."

"But senior year is absolutely *the best*. God, I had so much fun! Cheerleading. Student council. Senior trip. *Prom.* You're going to love it; I know you will." She wipes her forehead with the back of her forearm and then pauses. "There's so much to do. So much I want to see you do," she adds.

"Yup, I really do think they're going to make me head cheerleader this year," Mari says.

Her mom ignores her. "Do you know who you want to ask you to prom yet?"

"I'd sooner walk into a lake."

"What about *Dante*?"

"Sheesh, cool your jets, Mom. I tell you what—you can go in my place."

"I guarantee you'll get excited once we start dress shopping . . . and you know, you really should start letting me give you a few style tips. You're such a beautiful girl. A few small adjustments and you'll have to fight the boys off with a stick."

"I think I had that nightmare once," Mari says. "Need me to cut anything else?"

"You really should start dating. It'd be good for you."

"Let it go, Mom."

Her mom's eyes brighten. "What about Archie?"

"I have a knife."

"Fine." She puts her hands up in surrender. "I just want to make sure you're happy."

"Cutting things makes me happy."

"Then here," her mom says, handing her a head of romaine lettuce.

They work in comfortable silence for the next few minutes. There is no conversation, just the sounds of the kitchen. From the living room, a crowd erupts on the television. Mari's dad lets out a happy shout. Yay, sports.

"You read that letter yet?" her mom asks.

Mari sets down the knife and looks up at the ceiling. She wants to make her mom happy, but she's sick of this topic. She wants to scream at the top of her lungs. She wants to scream so loudly that it will shatter glass, send birds to flight, and set off car alarms.

Instead she drops her eyes to the chopped lettuce. "I don't care about contacting that woman, Mom. She's a stranger. You've always been here for me. I want to be here for you. What's wrong with that?"

Her mom sighs. "Nothing, honey. Just don't forget that there are other people out there that need you, too."

If I Could, I Would Hug You Back

THURSDAY

Mari clicks through the search results. All the first several websites are laid out in the same way. Neutral or light color schemes meant to exude reassurance. A large, happy logo on the main page. Links on the left-hand side that lead to sections that explain the basic information, the process of diagnosis, the treatment options, support group information.

The survival rates.

Mari reads page after page about fatty tissues, mammary glands, the lactiferous sinus, and lymphatic nodes. She encounters clunky medical terms, words like *metastasize, lobular carcinoma, chemoembolization*. They all sound like demons in some fantasy game. She whispers the words quietly over and over again, until they flow from her lips, hoping that mastering their names removes their power.

She studies illustrated diagrams of naked female torsos. The beige skin is always lifted from one breast to expose the spidery web of ligaments and ducts radiating from the beneath the nipple. She watches 3D-animation videos that show malevolent, black and purple lumps growing and spreading and then invading other parts of the body. She examines post-mastectomy photographs wherein single breasts hang asymmetrically opposite scars that look like crooked smiles. Mari is certain she will never be able to see another female—or herself—in the same way ever again.

Mari starts to recognize the same information and the same pictures on website after website. On the search results pages she skips past the links to medical sites and eventually stumbles across a blog kept by a woman diagnosed with stage four breast cancer.

Besides detailing her experiences with various treatments and describing how the disease affects her everyday life, the woman reflects in a way only the dying are really able to, recounting her accomplishments, noting her regrets, and offering advice. The writer, a mother of three, mostly posts about how much she loves her children. She writes with words of pain and love, of beauty and sadness.

To her children, she writes, "I pray not that you will be happy or successful. But that you will be good. That you will learn to lose your selves and lift up others."

Mari writes those words on her wall and then continues to read every other post, falling in love with the woman's wit and humility in struggle. The final post, written by the woman's husband, over two years ago, thanks readers for their support and provides the funeral information.

When there is no Next link to click anymore, Mari finally loses it. She takes off her glasses and buries her face in her arms and sobs for the first time since her mom broke the news to her.

Mari cries for this woman she did not know, this woman who has been in the earth for over two years. She cries for the woman's husband, for the woman's children. She cries for her own mom's future, bleak and blurry.

After a long time, she runs out of tears. Exhausted, she finds a tissue and blows her nose several times. She puts her glasses back on.

Macadamia comes over as if to comfort Mari. She nuzzles into her and licks the back of Mari's hand. Mari hugs her and then imagines the dog saying, "If I could, I would hug you back."

Mari suddenly wants to leave. Or she wants somebody to come over. Her parents had taken her brothers to the aquarium for the day, and Mari does not want to be alone. Dante is the only one of her friends she feels comfortable enough to open up to, but he's working.

Then she remembers Archie's text. She feels a pang of guilt that nearly a day has passed and she has not replied to it.

can you come over right now? She finally texts back.

Her phone immediately chirps with a reply: *how many condoms should i bring? j/k! on my way :)*

Despite his perverted joke, his text actually makes Mari feel better because it reminds her that someone is there for her. While she waits for Archie's arrival, she lies back in her bed and considers the difference between happiness and success and goodness.

All at once, the rain begins. It thrums upon the roof, patters against the windows. The wind howls. Mari goes to her window to watch the storm, perhaps the summer's last. Charcoal clouds mute the light. Trees sway. A single bird flits across the sky. An empty garbage can skitters across the street.

It's a mesmerizing sight, a reminder of nature's strength and beauty. Mari hopes Archie will arrive safely. The wind is strong, and he does not weigh that much.

A few minutes later, though, she spots him coming down the end of her street. He is umbrella-less and soaked through. As he gets closer, she notices that he is smiling to himself. It's kind of strange.

Mari waits for the doorbell, but it never chimes. Finally, she heads downstairs, grabbing a towel on her way. She pulls open the front door. He is just standing there like a creepster.

She invites him in and gives him some clean clothes that he changes into.

She makes some popcorn.

They watch an episode of *Firefly*.

They talk about the episode.

All of it is such a nice change of pace. It's like stepping from shadow into sunlight. She finally stops worrying about whether she should contact her biological mother; she stops worrying about what will happen with her mom. She just loses herself in the show, in the conversation, in Archie.

She moves closer to him on the couch.

Concerns about death and loss fall away. She wonders if she's starting to like Archie Walker.

It's such a weird possibility—her and Archie. She's never really considered it before. If anything, she had always thought of Sam, Dante, and Archie as family. Not close family. More like cousins.

Archie?

He is smart and kind of cute in a dorky way. Into the same stuff as her. He had even shown up wearing a Ravenclaw T-shirt, before he changed into the dry set of clothes she gave him—she'd always thought Ravenclaw would be her house if she attended Hogwarts.

But he was also . . . Archie. Immature. Kind of self-absorbed. A little too obsessed with math and school.

She could do worse. Maybe. She'd never really dated anyone before.

She moves even closer to him on the couch. Just a few inches away. She wonders if he notices. She smiles, asks if he wants to watch the next episode. Who knows how close they might be by the end of the night.

"There's nothing more I'd rather do. In fact," he says, turning to her and putting on a mock evil face, "I would kill my own mother to continue watching this show with you."

And even though Mari knows it's just a joke, all of her concerns return in a rush, like water busting through a damn. She drops her face into her hands and starts sobbing.

It's so embarrassing, to lose it like a crazy person out of nowhere, for a reason Archie can't possibly understand. But it's out of her control. She can't stop thinking about her mom dying. She can't stop feeling guilty that she tried not to think about it for even just a couple of hours, that she let herself worry over something stupid like a boy. She can't stop.

Archie apologizes and leaves in such a hurry that he forgets to take his clothes from the dryer.

Mari goes up to her room, closes the door, and lies face down on her bed.

She is alone again. But she still doesn't want to be. She musters enough energy to push herself off the bed, grab her keys, and head out the door.

Mari pulls the car into an empty space in the McCluck's parking lot, the windshield wipers swinging madly. The fluorescent interior of the fast food restaurant glows through the darkness and the rain. Only a few people are inside. She doesn't see Dante at the register and figures he must be on the fryers.

Mari kills the engine and clicks off the lights and wipers. The synchronous *squeak-whoosh-thump* ceases. Mari's world is swallowed by the sound of the rain drumming upon the car. The water streams down the windshield, blurring her view of McCluck's until it melts into a distorted blob of light.

She grabs her umbrella and places her hand on the door handle, but she does not open it.

She reassures herself that Dante is the right person to ask for advice about Archie, about her mom, about contacting her birth mother. After all, he was her first real friend.

In the beginning of the sixth grade, the science teacher had partnered her with Dante, the only other black kid in class. He had been gigantic even then. Mari had sighed, assuming she had just been paired with some idiotic jock.

They were supposed to be using the scientific method to experiment with how different shapes of paper airplanes would fly. Most of the kids in the class were having a blast, launching their planes across the room and disregarding the actual assignment.

For several minutes she and Dante sat eyeing the directions page between them. Dante didn't say anything, so Mari directed him to make the planes while she recorded the results. Dante set to folding the first plane while Mari took out her story notebook and began to write.

Dante peeked over her shoulder. "What are you writing?"

His voice was so deep it sounded like it belonged to someone twice his age. Yet at the same time, he spoke like a turtle poking its head from its shell.

"A story." Mari turned away then, protecting the page with her arm. "Why'd you stop making the plane?"

"With like spaceships and aliens?"

Mari had pretended to continue writing. "No."

"Dragons and stuff?"

"No. I write like real life. Only different."

Crestfallen, Dante went back to quietly folding planes.

But then Mari turned back toward Dante. "Do you write those kind of stories?"

"I don't write stories. I can't. But I met some friends, and they want to play this old game one of them read about."

"A video game or a board game?"

"Um, neither, I guess. You just make it up."

"So there aren't any rules?"

"There are," Dante said, carefully lining up his next fold.

"Then I don't get it." Mari said. "How do you play?"

"Like I said, you make it up. First, you create characters. Then the Dungeon Master—that's the person in charge—comes up with adventures. Then the players have to follow the game rules to beat the quests."

"So it's like the Dungeon Master versus everyone else?"

"Kind of, but not really," Dante said.

"Huh? Isn't the Dungeon Master just trying to come up with an adventure that the players can't beat?"

"No. If the adventure is too hard then it wouldn't be fun. Same if it's too easy. He has to make it so that it's in between."

Mari thought about this for a second and then asked, "Why does the Dungeon Master have to be a *he*?"

Dante shrugged. "He doesn't."

"So why do you keep saying *he*?"

Dante shrugged again.

"If you can do almost anything, how do you ever know what to do?"

"Archie says you we just figure it out together."

"What's to stop someone from just going off on her own and making stupid decisions?" Mari asked.

"Nothing, I guess."

"And there's no screen or board or anything?"

"Not really." Dante turned the paper over and folded it again.

"So, like, the game happens in your imagination? Like a video game without a console?"

"Yeah."

"That's weird."

Dante's face reddened. He finished folding the plane and quietly said, "I guess."

"Good weird, though." Mari looked down at her notebook. "Maybe I could be the person who makes up the stories. The Dungeon Lord."

"Dungeon Master."

"Whatever."

Dante smiled at Mari, held out the plane for her to take. "I'll check with Archie, Sam, and Sarah."

"What are they like?" Mari asked, taking the plane and turning it over to examine its structural integrity. She was impressed by the precision of the folds.

"Archie's really smart and funny. You'll love him. Sam can be kind of quiet, but he's cool. Sarah is pretty nice."

"Well, I'll start making up some stories with swords and stuff. But if this turns out to be lame, I'm not going to keep doing it."

"Okay," Dante said. "Maybe Archie can give you the rule book today and we can start playing next week."

"What? He just, like, carries it around with him?"

"Yeah."

Mari put away her story notebook and made a mental note to read a few fantasy novels soon. She handed the plane back to Dante and turned her attention to the science worksheet. She wrote their names on it and then told Dante, "You're clear for takeoff."

Dante tossed the plane like a dart and it swooped left, smashed into the side of a table, and fell to the floor. "Oops," he said as he picked it up and tried to straighten its crumpled nose. "I hate my hands. They're too big."

A thunderclap shakes the world, interrupting Mari's memory. She considers the rain, considers how much she will tell Dante.

She counts to three in her head and then in a fluid motion pulls the door handle, pops open her umbrella, steps into the rain, and slams the door shut.

The sound of the falling water magnifies. More thunder rumbles in the distance. She steps quickly through the shallow lake that the parking lot has become, her umbrella insufficient.

She walks in and approaches a Hispanic kid at the counter whose arms are covered in tattoos.

"Hi," she says.

"S'up, Mami?" he says.

"Can I speak with Dante, please?"

"He's not here," the kid says. "But you can speak with me." He winks.

Mari ignores it. "I thought he works Thursdays?"

"He took off."

"Did he say where he was going?"

He shrugs.

She sighs. "Well, thanks, anyways."

She pulls her hood back up. Opens her umbrella. Takes a deep breath and plunges back into the rain alone, feeling like a diver dropping into the ocean.

When Mari looks up, she's surprised by stars. There are so many it makes her dizzy. They fill the black sky, clusters of light denser in some areas than others, but all shining through the eons to reach her. Most are pinpricks of white, but some blink a pale blue or orange. Behind them, the magnificent swath of the galaxy's cloudy center stretches across the heavens like some cosmic gash. Underlining it all, the silhouette of a tree line spans the horizon, backlit by some unseen city.

"It's beautiful," Mari says as if she were in some cathedral.

Archie puts his arm around Mari and pulls her closer. "I know."

She rests her head on his chest and takes his hand in hers. She holds it as if it were a bird that might fly away.

A chilly breeze blows over their hill, rustling the surrounding trees and grass. She draws warmth from Archie's body. The blanket beneath them tickles the band of exposed skin below the hem of her sweatshirt. She rolls onto her side still holding Archie's hand.

Mari closes her eyes. "I'm afraid I'll fall in."

"I won't let you," he says.

Mari leans in to kiss him, but her lips only find air. She opens her eyes and sees that she's alone.

Above, the sky starts to turn. The stars rotate, anchored to the Northern Star, accelerating with each second. It's as if the Earth is a globe spun by a child.

Mari panics. She reaches out only to remember that nobody is there. She flattens her back against the ground. Stretches her arms out to her sides and grips fistfuls of grass.

It's no use. She's slipping.

She feels the centrifugal force pulling her into space. Her body rises from the ground, just barely at first, but then higher and higher. The grass she holds rips from out of the ground, soil crumbling from the nests of tiny roots. She opens her hands. The grass clumps fall. Loose green blades flutter downward.

Mari closes her eyes. She feels her body ascending, floating upward and outward. She opens her eyes. The sky is now spinning so quickly that the stars have become white streaks of concentric circles.

Mari wakes. The world is still. Still dark. Still raining.

Still lonely.

Dante

Endless Rows of Lonely Men

FRIDAY

The homeless guy drops a few sweaty, crumpled dollar bills in front of Dante. He then digs into his pocket and lets a handful of coins clatter onto the counter next to the cash.

"How much was it again?" the man asks, his voice raw.

Dante scoops up the money and returns it to the man. "Don't worry about it," he says. "I got you."

The man smiles at Dante, his teeth crooked and yellow. "Thank you, young man."

He steps aside to wait for his food, and it's not long before Dante returns with a bag stuffed full of fried chicken. The man thanks Dante again and then heads back into the night.

Dante checks the clock. Just a few minutes left before he can lock up. But then he still has to wipe down the tables, put up the chairs, and mop the floor.

He yawns. Rolls his shoulders. Adjusts the notorious McCluck's hat that sits upon his head. It is notorious because the hat is in the shape of a foam chicken, complete with a comb dangling from each side of the beak. The dangling combs look like a pair of red testicles to everyone except, apparently, the person who designed the hat.

Dante is hoping that was the last customer of the night when three guys he recognizes from school walk in. Each wears loafers without socks, a different shade of khaki shorts, and some variation of a collared shirt with the sleeves rolled up revealing evenly tanned forearms and shiny watches. Their hair is all mussed in an artificial way and they wear sunglasses despite the fact that it's nighttime.

One of the guys approaches the register and flashes a smile, revealing perfect white teeth indicative of privilege and date rape. He reeks of alcohol. "Gimme a number seven with a diet Coke, bro. Hey, nice balls."

The guy reaches up and flicks one of the combs. It sways back and forth. His friends crack up. Dante sighs. Even though he's got at least one foot and a hundred pounds on the biggest guy of the group, Dante feels insignificant.

And he wonders at the fact that they haven't recognized him from school yet. It's not like there are that many linebacker-sized black guys lumbering through the hallways. In fact, there's just one. Probably too drunk, he figures.

"Would you like to Cluck-Up your order for only seventy-nine cents more?" Dante asks because he has to.

"What?"

"You know, upgrade to the next size."

The guy looks above Dante, considers the menu board as if it holds the answer. "Yeah, sure."

Dante punches the order into the register. "For here or to go?"

The guy holds his credit card out to Dante and doesn't answer the question. Instead, he turns back to his friends to resume their conversation. Dante punches the "To Go" button and then runs the card.

The other two order in the same manner and then stand to the side to wait for their food. He hurriedly fixes their orders, but can't help but overhear their conversation as he does so.

". . . No way, man."

"Yeah way, dude."

"Bro, I thought she was Chad's girl."

"Well, she wasn't with Chad when Charles and I were tapping that on her parents' bed tonight."

"Oh, man, what a megaslut!"

The three break out in guffawing laughter and high-fives.

Dante wonders what his own friends are up to. Certainly not "tapping" Chad's girlfriend on her parents' bed.

He fills their orders and calls their numbers. They grab the sacks and leave without saying thanks. Dante locks the door behind them. Removes his chicken hat. Starts working through the closing duties, all the while cursing his coworker Marco who never showed for his shift.

An hour later, Dante finishes counting the cash from the registers and then deposits it into the safe in the manager's office. He clicks off the lights, sets the alarm, and walks out.

Dante drinks in the fresh evening air. And before stepping into his car, he cranes his neck upward and gazes beyond the humming power lines and signs. He imagines distant galaxies. Galaxies where nobody wears chicken hats.

Or where chickens wear human hats.

Dante climbs the stairs carefully. He does not want to wake his grandparents who have been in bed for hours. Like usual, he takes a shower to try to wash away the scent of grease and fried chicken. He feels it's bad enough to be black and work at a fried chicken joint. He doesn't need to smell like the stuff.

After the shower, he returns to his room feeling wide awake. He considers the two PCs on his desk. One works. The other sits with its casing opened and circuitry exposed, like a patient in the middle of surgery.

After powering on the working computer, he glances at the crack under the door and confirms that the hallway is still dark. He listens for a moment, but hears nothing beyond the comforting hum of his computer.

Satisfied, he makes his way to a website he likes to visit while everyone else is fast asleep.

Above rows of attractive, smiling faces a headline proclaims *Hot singles in YOUR area might be searching for YOU right NOW!*

On his profile homepage, a small number two appears next to his mailbox icon. Intrigued, Dante clicks it.

The first message is from a user named Wonderboy24. Before reading the message, Dante examines the picture. The man, who appears older than both the number and the word "boy" that the username suggests, has sandy brown hair and retro wire-rim glasses. He has a square jaw and nice smile, but his eyes are too far apart and his nose seems too small for his face. Dante deletes the message without reading it.

The next message is from CuriousPhreek215. In his profile pic, CuriousPhreek215 is pulling a Phillies cap so low that the logo and brim take up three quarters of the shot. Beneath the brim are full lips and a closely trimmed beard. Dante does not fault CuriousPhreek215 for hiding his face, as he still hasn't put up a picture of himself. Dante opens the message.

yo i noticed u nt 2 far. wnt 2 mt 4 a fk? hmu.

Dante deletes the message.

His inbox clear, Dante begins browsing profiles.

Picture. Username. Hobbies.

This is the order in which Dante scans the endless rows of lonely men.

If he likes the picture, he looks at the username. If the username is acceptable, he examines the hobbies. If the hobbies are acceptable, he clicks on the profile and reads more about the person. Straight lurking. As superficial as it gets.

He has never met up with anyone.

He has never contacted anyone.

He just searches, excited and scared about a world he's long known he belongs to but has never had the courage to enter, not even virtually.

After about half an hour, he has scanned approximately fifteen pages of search results, twenty-five profile pics per page. He's just about to log out when he notices that a new message has appeared in his user inbox.

The profile picture is the anonymous male outline that Dante also uses. The username reads Takei4Life. Annoyed by the lack of image but intrigued by the handle, Dante opens the message.

Hi DeeThreepio,

How are you? I read your profile and was really interested to see that we share a love for technology—I also built my own computer (I'm actually a programmer). But what I really liked was what you wrote in your biography. It was honest and sweet, and it really resonated with me. It felt like something I would write, even though I didn't think of it myself (I hope that doesn't sound weird—I'm just trying to say that maybe we have a lot in common on a deeper level, too). Even though you're not looking for a relationship right now, how about a friendship? I've been really lonely lately and could use a friend. Maybe you could also?

Dante moves his cursor over the Delete button. He pauses. He rereads the message. Instead of deleting it, he types a brief reply.

Hi, Takei4Life. Maybe I could.

Dante hesitates. Then, clicks Send.

Immediately, he feels his face warm and his heart rate quicken. He moves the cursor to close the window, but then his inbox notifies him that there's already a new reply from Takei4Life.

Great :) How about coffee this Thur? The coffee shop @ 16th & Walnut. 7:30pm.

Dante's heart thrums.

Suddenly, he hears movement in the hallway. He minimizes the browser just as someone opens his door. His grandpa's face peeks inside, eyelids drooping.

"Still up?" he asks.

Dante's heart races. "Just gaming," he lies.

"Well, it's late. Get to bed, now. Don't forget your auntie and uncle are coming over in the morning."

His grandpa pulls the door shut. Dante listens to his steps recede. A few moments later, he hears the toilet flush, more footsteps, and then a door close.

Dante reopens the browser.

He types a reply.

See you then ;)

Quiet That Forms in Their Wake

SATURDAY

Dante hears the front door open. The shuffle of footsteps. Voices rattling off greetings. The sounds of his uncle's family arriving. Not yet prepared to deal with his overly exuberant twin cousins, Dante remains in bed.

But as soon as the scent of frying bacon hits his nose, Dante's out of bed and heading downstairs.

He finds his grandma at the stove and his grandpa sitting at the table in his usual spot with the newspaper folded over his knee. Dante's Uncle Jason and Aunt Jewel sit on the other side of the table. His little cousins, Andre and D'Andre, are running around the backyard in the sunlight. One chases the other with a neon orange plastic Wiffle ball bat.

"Morning, sunshine," his grandma says over her shoulder.

His grandpa nods.

"My, my, who's this fine young man?" his Aunt Jewel says, standing and motioning for Dante to come in for a hug.

Dante embraces her, inhaling the combined scent of her perfume, lotion, and hair burnt from straightening. "Hi, Auntie Jewel."

She kisses him on the cheek.

"S'up, Dante?" his uncle asks.

"Not much, Uncle J. Nice to see you guys again." They shake, and after his uncle is done trying to crush every bone in his hand, Dante sits in front of a waiting plate of food.

"So. Senior year," his uncle says, smiling. He is, no doubt, recalling his own eighteen-year-old exploits. Dante presumes that they were probably a far cry from what his own will be.

"Yup," Dante says.

Still smiling, his uncle takes a sip of his coffee and then asks, "You taking some tough classes this year to get you ready for college?"

"The usual."

"What's your GPA?" his uncle asks.

"Three point one."

"Not bad, not bad. But you got to work on that this year, man. Crack down on those books so you can get a nice scholarship. Know what I mean?"

"You shush, now," Dante's aunt says and kisses him on the forehead. "The boy's doing just fine—and he knows computers. How many times has he fixed yours?"

"For real. D's like a black Bill Gates. Still, I know Mom and Pops would appreciate him getting a full ride."

"Amen," Dante's grandfather says.

His grandma turns toward them. "Oh, just ignore them, Dante. You get into the school you want, and we'll find a way to make it work. Besides, your daddy's military benefits should cover most of it."

His uncle changes the subject. "Hey, you going to go out for football this year? Pops been telling me about his phone ringing off the hook from Coach."

"Shoot," his grandpa says. "Man won't stop begging me to get Dante out on that field since this is last chance. Said the sheer size of the boy in full gear would bring scouts from at least a few Division II and Division III schools eager to capitalize upon that potential."

Dante keeps his eyes on his plate, "Football's not really my thing, Uncle J."

"Yeah, I know, I know. Wasn't mine neither. That didn't stop Pops from forcing me to play." He slaps the old man on the shoulder.

Dante's grandpa chuckles. "You should have seen this boy out there on that field, Dante. Nobody—and I mean nobody—could sit on a bench like him!"

Everyone laughs, even Uncle Jason. "Ain't that the truth! That was your daddy's game." He tilts his chin in the direction of the mantle in the living room where Dante's dad's MVP trophy sits from the year his team won the state championship. "Damn, D. You should have seen him out on that field. Built like a Mack truck. Just like you. Dudes was so scared of him barreling down that field, they didn't even try to tackle him. Just stepped right out the way!"

Everyone laughs again at the memory, even Dante. He had seen a few of the tapes. And even though he couldn't care less about the sport, he would give anything to have been able to see his dad play in real life.

"But ain't no matter," his uncle continues. "I was the brother the head cheerleader had her eye on."

Aunt Jewel winks at her husband and then turns to Dante. "So how 'bout you? Who you got your eye on?"

Dante examines his toast like it's the most interesting thing in the world. "Nobody, really."

"Not even that light-skinned girl with those pretty eyes you be playing games with all the time? What's her name?"

"Mari," his grandma answers as she sets down a plate of sizzling bacon onto the middle of the table.

Dante grabs a piece. "Nah. Not my type."

"Well, don't worry, honey," his aunt says. "You sweet as can be. Girls will appreciate that more the older you get. The right girl's out there just waiting for you to find her."

"I kind of doubt that," Dante says.

Before anyone can inquire further about Dante's romantic endeavors, something—rather, someone—slams into the sliding glass doors that open into the backyard, making everyone jump.

The twins press their faces into the glass, one squishing his nose flat and crossing his eyes, the other putting his mouth on the glass and inflating his cheeks to display all of his teeth and gums. They drag the door open and burst into the kitchen, a whirlwind of energy. They immediately begin jumping on Dante's back, vying for a perch atop his mountainous shoulders.

"What's up, guys?" Dante says, resigned to his fate.

"Hey, Dante!" Andre or D'Andre says.

"S'up, cuz!" D'Andre or Andre says.

Dante could never tell the difference.

His Uncle Jason puts down his coffee mug and glares at the twins. "Yo—cut that out. Sit down and let the man finish his breakfast. Then you can climb him."

Aunt Jewel pulls out two nearby chairs. "Andre, D'Andre, babies, I made you some plates. Have a seat and eat now."

They stop climbing on Dante and follow her directions.

"I want french fries," one says.

"Me too," says the other.

"Well, this ain't no restaurant," Dante's grandpa says.

The twins begin pounding their fists on the table in unison. *"French fries! French fries! French fries!"*

Uncle Jason puts his hands atop theirs to cease the noise. "Grandma cooked you guys some delicious food so least you can do is eat it. Once you finish half your plates, you can go play."

"Won't take but a minute for me to make them some fries if they can sit still that long," Dante's grandma says as she reaches into the freezer.

"Can we go on Dante's computer?" one asks.

"No," Dante says.

His grandma points the greasy spatula at Dante. "When Jesus was in Bethsaida and that big ol' crowd came to him, you think he kept those five loaves of bread and two pieces of fish all to himself? No, sirree. He shared that bit of food and fed five thousand people with it. You think if the Son of God were on Earth with us today, he'd tell someone they couldn't go on his computer?"

"Fine," Dante sighs. He grabs another piece of bacon to console himself.

And just like that, the twins are off to Dante's room.

Everyone enjoys the peace and quiet that forms in their wake. They eat their breakfast and sip their coffees in silence for a bit, and then conversation gradually resumes. They talk about Uncle Jason's new teaching job downtown. Somebody retiring. Somebody's new baby that everyone agrees is ugly. Aunt Jewel's candle-making business.

And then the twins reappear in the kitchen. Grins stretch across their faces. Their eyes are wide and swing between Dante and their parents. They say nothing but look like they're about to burst.

Everyone turns, waiting for them to speak.

But each just keeps prodding the other.

"Out with it," Uncle Jason finally says.

"Dante likes boys!" they shout at the same time and then erupt in a fit of giggles.

Everyone turns to Dante. He feels like he's on an operating table with his chest split open for surgery.

"Now what you two going on about?" Aunt Jewel asks.

"Come see!" they say and then dart out of the kitchen toward Dante's room.

"What they talking about, D?" Uncle Jason asks.

Once again, everyone looks at Dante, expecting him to explain. But he can't speak. He can't breathe. He feels lightheaded and nauseous, like he's either going to pass out or throw up. He just shakes his head like he has no idea. But suddenly he remembers. Last night, after browsing the dating site, he didn't clear his browser history. They must have pulled up the site somehow.

To his horror, everyone rises, their chairs scraping back at the same time. They all head upstairs.

Except for Dante. He remains at the table with the last piece of bacon, too sick to his stomach to eat it.

To Strengthen Us

SUNDAY

When church ends and everyone scoots out of the pews, Dante's grandpa grips his arm and steers him down a hallway toward the pastor's office. His grandma follows. Nobody says anything.

They arrive while the pastor is still in the sanctuary chatting with the other members of his flock, so they wait outside his office door. Dante leans back against the wall, staring at his ill-fitting shoes. His grandpa folds his arms over his chest and reads the announcements posted to the bulletin board in the hallway. His grandma stands with her eyes closed and hands clasped together.

After some time, the church clears out and Pastor Paul approaches them. He ushers them into his office. It is a cramped, windowless space. Only a simple wooden cross hangs on the faded yellow walls. Papers clutter the desk around a large computer with a beige casing. Dante wonders if it even works. The pastor finds his seat behind the desk. His grandparents sit in the only two visitor chairs, and Dante stands behind them.

Dante's grandpa then recounts what the twins found on Dante's computer the previous day. The rows of men. Dante's profile. Dante's refusal to deny any of it. His grandpa's words drip with shame.

Dante's heart races. He prepares himself for what's to come. He knows the arguments that will probably be made, the Bible verses that will probably be quoted. He knows it all. During his years of confusion, he'd read them all dozens, if not hundreds, of times. He'd read the commentary and the debates and made up his mind. He's been secretly preparing for this moment for years, and he is ready to refute anything if need be.

Pastor Paul takes a deep breath and then touches the tips of his fingers together like a steeple. He leans forward and meets Dante's eyes. He looks profoundly disappointed.

"You are not a homosexual, Dante," the pastor says in his sonorous Nigerian accent.

His grandma starts crying quietly, and all the fight leaves Dante. He drops his eyes to the floor. He examines the carpet tiles, a visual white noise of patternless flooring meant to mask stains. "I'm not?"

"You are *not* a homosexual, Dante."

"Um."

"God does not make homosexuals, Dante. You are being tempted by the Devil. You must overcome these temptations, Dante."

Dante shifts his weight to his other foot. He swallows hard. He wonders why the pastor keeps saying his name. "Why would God do that?" he asks after a few moments.

"God tempts us to strengthen us, Dante. Fire forges steel. Struggle forges souls."

Dante considers this for a few moments. He does not disagree on that point.

"You can overcome these temptations, Dante—with prayer, with the support and love of your grandparents, with Jesus. 'With God all things are possible.' Matthew. Chapter nineteen. Verse twenty-six."

Dante nods.

"How should we punish him?" his grandpa asks.

The pastor exhales. "Hate the sin, love the sinner. You must continue to love this child. Jesus still loves Dante, and Jesus does not want the Devil to win Dante's soul. Pray for Dante, and watch over Dante. Do what you can to shield Dante from temptation. This is a battle with eternal consequences, a battle Dante cannot afford to lose."

His grandpa nods. "No computer."

Dante looks up, hating that everyone is talking about him as if he weren't even there, as if he were a gremlin. "Why is it a sin?" he asks, working up at least some measure of defiance.

His grandpa looks taken aback at the question, but Pastor Paul maintains his composure. He waits a beat before responding, and when he does, his words are slow and somber, like mourners walking home from a funeral. "'Thou shalt not lie with mankind, as with womankind: it is abomination.' Leviticus. Chapter eighteen. Verse twenty-two. Let us lay hands on this child."

As if that completely settles it, his pastor and grandparents all rise. They put their hands on Dante's shoulders and bow their heads. Dante keeps his eyes open. He stares at a crack in the wall.

"Dear, Lord," the pastor begins. "Here is a beloved son. We raise him up to You. We ask that You bless him. Give him the wisdom to walk the righteous path. Give him the strength to resist temptation. Give him the courage to be whom You created him to be. In the name of Jesus Christ, Our Lord and Savior. Amen."

"Amen," Dante says.

You Made Me Strong, But I Am Weak

MONDAY

"I'm gay," Dante tells his friends.

In his head.

In real life, he stands at the sliding glass doors of Mari's house and gazes into the backyard of the neighbor's house. A bunch of little kids are playing some chaotic form of football. One of them tosses the ball high into the air, and the others fight to catch it. The one who succeeds then runs the ball back to an imaginary goal line while everybody else tries to tackle him.

Mari and Archie sit at the table talking about something. Dante takes slow, controlled breaths. His arms are folded over his chest to still his hands from shaking. For the last half hour he has been mentally declaring his sexuality, ready to make the announcement once Sam and Sarah arrive, even though they never usually talked about stuff like this as a group.

But it does not look like Sam and Sarah will ever arrive.

As he continues watching the kids, Dante can't help but remember "Smear the Queer," a game most of the boys liked to play back when he was in grade school. Whoever had the football ran about in order to avoid getting tackled by the others for as long as possible. Once taken down, the kid would toss the ball to someone else, and that person became the "queer" who everyone else tried to "smear."

Like wolves targeting the weakest in the herd, the boys had always measured the look of fear upon the receiver's face and the amount of tears streaming down his cheeks post-tackle. Those deemed the weakest would be thrown the ball most frequently, as they provided the most entertainment.

It was a malicious game that could only be the product of childhood or the medieval age.

Dante never liked to play it and was glad that the other boys seemed to naturally fear him. Nobody wanted to be tackled by the big, black kid. Dante spent most recesses wandering up and down the playground scanning the gravel for unusual stones that he could add to his rock collection.

But one day the ball had sailed through someone's hands and landed at Dante's feet. He picked it up to toss it back as he heard someone bellow, *"Smear the queer!"*

Caught in the frenzy of the game and finding confidence in numbers, the boys ignored their natural fear of Dante. They rushed toward him.

Dante froze.

They smashed into him. He saw sky and then a flash of red as the back of his head smacked concrete. Bodies piled onto him, crowding out the sky and crushing his lungs. Anonymous fists pummeled his body.

He struggled to breathe. Bright bursts of pain flashed in a hundred different places.

He saw a patch of blue emerge between the crush of bodies and, as if by instinct, he flung the ball through the gap. As quickly as they had descended upon him, the frenzy departed. Dante was left a crumpled mess of tears and bruises.

He waited for the paraprofessional who monitored the playground to rush to his aid, but the man was known for turning a blind eye to the brutality of the children. He believed that such torment built character.

After some time, Dante pushed himself up and slowly moved into a sitting position. He wiped the wetness from his eyes with dusty hands. He pulled up his shirt and examined his torso to ensure that all internal organs remained internal. He touched the back of his head and was relieved when he did not find blood.

Dante did not stand and sprint toward revenge. Neither did he seek a teacher to tell. Instead, aching and convinced that half the bones in his body were broken, he rolled onto all fours and searched the ground for the rocks he had dropped when the ball had fallen into his path.

The other kids left him alone for the remainder of that recess, but word of his softness spread through the school in whispers and giggles. Boys were not supposed to be soft. Big boys were definitely not supposed to be soft. And big, black boys were not even supposed to say the word "soft."

They relished his weakness. It became the whetstone against which they sharpened their own inflated senses of strength and self-worth.

They started to go out of their way to throw him the ball whenever they played. Even if he wasn't playing, even though he never wanted to play.

If he were at the opposite end of the playground, sitting in the shade of some tree looking at leaves shifting in the wind, they would work their game in his direction and toss him the ball.

Even if he didn't pick it up, they would still rush over and dog-pile him. Sometimes he would run. Slow and uncoordinated, his attempts at escape only elicited additional mockery later as they reenacted the sad scene.

Dante usually just picked up the ball, closed his eyes, and braced for impact.

I'm sorry, he would pray as he waited for the flurry to crash into him. *Jesus, I'm sorry you made me strong, but I am weak.*

So Dante stopped going outside for recess. Instead, every day he'd beg the teacher to let him stay inside and use one of the computers. Probably sensing the real issue, she always let him.

The sound of Archie's die bouncing across the table brings Dante back to the present.

"I'm calling it," Mari says.

Dante considers just telling Archie and Mari right now. He could always talk to Sam and Sarah later. But that doesn't feel right. He wants to tell all of his friends at once, to deal with all of their reactions at once. He decides to wait until Wednesday.

"Okay," he says.

Water and Air

TUESDAY

Dante lowers himself into the pool. He feels his body, buoyed by the water, grow lighter. It is one of his favorite feelings in the world.

He stands at the end of his lane, soothed by the water's gentle swaying. As he begins stretching, he watches the handful of other midday swimmers. In the next lane, a middle-aged Indian guy wearing a black Speedo, black goggles, and blue swim cap breast-strokes lap after lap like a machine. On the other side of him, a white woman backstrokes steadily. At the far end of the pool, three elderly people walk back and forth across the shallow end like aquatic somnambulists.

His grandfather had taken him to the gym, perhaps hoping it would boost Dante's masculinity. But Dante headed straight for the pool. He's never competed, but he has always found that the activity of swimming calmed him. Underwater, it is quiet, the real world light-years away.

Dante pulls on his goggles, takes a deep breath, and lowers himself beneath the water's surface. He kicks off the wall. His body cuts through the fluid world, and then a moment later he breaks the surface and begins a functional forward crawl, tilting his head every three or four strokes to suck in air. He revels in the reprieve from gravity. He reaches the end of the lane, and because he has never learned to flip-turn, he merely turns around, takes a deep breath, lowers himself into the water, and kicks off the wall again.

Dante spends the first several laps focusing on his breathing so that he does not drown. But after a few laps, he finds a rhythm and tries to free his mind.

But instead of reaching a meditative state, he is gripped by anxiety. After church, his grandpa had forced him to box up his PCs and take them to the basement. It was like burying old friends.

He swims. His thoughts find a rhythm. In spite of the punishment, in spite of the feeling that he has once again disappointed his grandparents—and his father—he discovers something like freedom in being outed, in no longer having to hide the truth from his family. He just wishes he had walked out of the closet instead of being shoved.

At least he could control how he'd tell his friends. He should have just told them last night. What was he afraid of?

Archie was logical. Mari was empathetic. Sam was laid back. Sarah was open-minded.

He can't see a universe in which any of his friends will reject him based on this new truth.

But still. Something holds him back.

Maybe he simply resents the horrible awkwardness of it all. He hates that the world makes coming out such a big deal. It's not like straight people have to muster up the courage to proclaim their heterosexuality. Nobody feels the pressure to announce their hair color, their height, their favorite snack food. How ridiculous to have to admit—as if you were a drug addict or an alcoholic—that you are naturally attracted to the same sex.

But he knows that he cannot change the world. That he cannot control how other people react. He can only do his thing and let everyone else sort through their own feelings. Worse comes to worst, he moves to San Francisco.

Dante suddenly feels short of breath. He notices that he's swimming at too fast a pace to sustain. He focuses on the tiled, blue line at the bottom of the pool and tries to slip back into a relaxing rhythm, pulling his arms through water and air, water and air.

Dante swims several more laps before pausing for a break. He pulls the goggles off his head and looks around to find that he is alone in the pool.

Indian guy. White woman. Old people. All have gone.

The sloshing water and Dante's labored breathing echo, trapped by walls and water.

Exploding and Reforming

WEDNESDAY

Dante's spirit deflates as he reads the text from Mari. No Magic. She probably still hasn't heard from Sam and Sarah. His plan ruined, Dante starts to wonder if the universe is trying to tell him not to bother.

Sick of the universe, he gets in his car and drives over to Sam's.

He knocks on the door, ready to drag Sam over to Mari's so he can make his stupid announcement and be done with it. And then they can play their game.

A moment later, Grace, Sam's little sister, opens the door.

"Sam's not here," she says.

"Who is it?" Sam's mom calls from within.

"Dante," Grace answers over her shoulder.

"Who?"

"Sam's black friend. The big one."

"Oh."

Dante's not sure how he feels about this exchange. Why couldn't she have said, "Sam's nice friend?" or even, "Sam's friend who's good with computers?" Why must he always be reduced to the things that he cannot control? Unfortunately, he is certain that soon enough he will be known to others as "that big, black, gay guy."

He sighs. "Do you know where he is?"

"I don't know. You could check the playground."

"Okay, thanks."

"Yup," she says as she closes the door.

Dante drives to the elementary school. He parks in the empty lot under an orange street lamp, gets out, and walks over to the playground. The place seems empty.

He circles it a couple times to confirm that there's nobody else there beside himself. He must have missed Sam.

Dante climbs to the top of one of the slides and sits down. He tilts his head to the stars. They seem so still, so peaceful, but everything—everything—is exploding and reforming infinitely in every direction.

Crazy Orgies

THURSDAY

Tonight, Dante is supposed to meet a guy at a coffee shop downtown.

Unfortunately, he's also scheduled to work. A fact he'd overlooked last Friday night when he agreed to the plan. A plan he hasn't gotten around to cancelling yet.

To make matters worse, that morning his grandpa had declared that he was no longer allowed to drive until he conquered his temptations. He took Dante's keys and then handed him a small one that paired with a bike lock, just like Archie's. Like the pastor, his grandpa had quoted the Bible during the exchange. A verse about cutting off a hand and removing an eye.

His grandpa had also taken Dante's smartphone and presented him with a brick-like cell phone. It hailed from an era before social networking, before touchscreens and Wi-Fi. It could not access the Internet. It could not take pictures. It had an actual keypad and a small, greenish screen that displayed information in a boxy 8-bit text not designed to be nostalgic. Texting on it was more trouble than it was worth.

He had sadly concluded that the only thing the phone would be good for was calling people.

But as he bikes to work that afternoon, Dante tries to make the best of his situation. The phone? It can double as a self-defense weapon. No computer? Time to reconnect with the real world. The bike? Exercise. And a new perspective. The world looks different on a bike.

He sees more, such as the two-story houses and manicured, green lawns of his neighborhood giving way to ranch-style homes with patchy, brown lawns, busted chain link fences, and children's toys left outside. The sidewalk is as crooked as bad teeth.

He pedals out of the residential areas and begins passing strip malls comprised of payday loan places, liquor stores, and pawn shops. He passes an old, bearded, white guy plodding along the sidewalk while pulling a vacuum cleaner. A car driving in the opposite direction lowers its passenger side window and ejects a fast food bag that bulges with trash. The bag rolls a few times and then comes to rest in the gutter, which is full of shattered glass and cigarette butts.

Arriving at work, Dante hops off the bike. He looks around and notices for the first time that there is no bike rack. He locks it to a signpost, wipes the sweat from his forehead, and then slips on his uniform shirt and chicken hat. Dante enters the restaurant.

"Your old set of wheels crap out on you, son?" calls out Marco, a scrawny coworker whose arms are sleeved in tattoos.

"Something like that," he says, the truth too difficult to explain. "Hey, what was up last Friday?" Marco had been the no-show.

"Sorry about that, man. Had some stuff to take care of. You know how it is."

Dante does not. He clocks in, washes his hands, looks at the schedule to see what position the manager assigned him for the day, and then takes his place behind the fryers.

"So. S'up, Papi?" Marco asks.

Dante focuses his eyes on the red digital numbers that indicate the time remaining before he should take the chicken out of the oil. "Not much."

"Cool, cool. You guys start up next week, too?" Marco goes to the other high school, the one on the same side of the highway as McCluck's.

"Yup. Tuesday."

"School is some broke-ass, shit, man. I ain't never gonna use that stuff, real rap. But ya know what the weird thing is? I'm kind of glad to go back. I been bored as fuck these days. I just been smokin' and drinkin' and shit all day, playin' Xbox, shootin' hoops when it ain't too hot, gettin' my ass to work to fry up chicken for these fat fools, ya feel me?" He turns to the customer whose order he's punching into the register. "No offense, sir."

Marco turns back to Dante and continues. "At least at school I get to show off some fly-ass threads I bought this summer and bag me some pussy. Feel me?"

Again, Dante does not. Nonetheless, he feigns solidarity with a grunt of agreement.

"Your order number is forty-two, sir. It should be right up—but for real, Papi, this year you and me gotta chill, son. I'll introduce you to some black chicks, some back-to-Africa type chicks. I know you ain't got none of them at that fancy school you go to. I'm tellin' you, son, they'll put a smile on that sad, Eeyore-looking mit of yours. Ain't no way those skinny white bitches be enough for your big ass. And maybe you can hook a brother up with some of that preppy ass I know you must be gettin'. Some rich bitches, so I don't got to work no more. Some chick whose Daddy Moneybags owns some mansion on a beach. We could live there and walk along the beach and shit during the day, and I could watch the sun set over the waves and shit as she goes down on me. You and your new black chick can come over and we could get mad high and have crazy orgies, real rap—Good evening, Ma'am. How can I help you?"

Dante marvels at Marco's oddly poetic daydream. As alien as Marco seems to Dante, at least Marco had invited him to visit the imaginary beach house.

But how can he tell Marco that he does not want a girl, that it's another guy's arms he wants to feel around him? Would Marco still want to have "crazy orgies" with him?

Probably not.

The fryer beeps as the red numbers flash zero. Dante lifts the basket, lets the oil drip from the chicken for a few moments, and then dumps the sizzling pieces onto the trays under the heat lamps. He retrieves a new batch of floured chicken and begins the process anew.

Some vague sentiment in Marco's vision lingers in Dante's brain. Dante imagines himself on a beach at sunset. He smells the salt water. He hears the waves crashing. Seagulls cawing. He feels the warm sand pocked with tiny shells beneath his feet. Cool, foaming water running over his toes as it approaches and then recedes, approaches and recedes. His feet sink into the sand. He feels a hand grasp his.

Yes, he wants that.

"Hey, Marco?" Dante says.

Marco's wide eyes peek over the chicken. "Yeah, Papi?"

"I've got some stuff to take care of. Cover for me?" Dante removes his hat. The manager walks over and tells him to put it back on. But Dante tells him he's about to throw up, and the manager moves out of his way.

Marco stifles a laugh. "Real slick, D," Marco says once the manager is out of earshot. "What you really got goin' on?"

Dante punches out. "Meeting someone. Sorry to ditch you like this."

Marco waves away the apology. "You got me last Friday. Just do me one favor, all right?"

Skeptical, Dante asks what that favor might be.

"When you up in your girl later tonight, tell her to call you 'Marco.'"

Dante steps off the bus and then jogs through the rain to the coffee shop at the end of the block. He is drenched and short of breath when he steps through the door. His heart is a hummingbird.

There's a long line of customers in various states of soaked. The baristas scurry about behind a display case that contains only a few remaining pastries and expensive bottled drinks. Conversation fills the air, punctuated by bursts of noise from the grinder and steamer.

Dante scans the crowded tables. All the faces blur together. He curses the fact that he hadn't thought to ask Takei4Life for a picture.

He tries to focus on finding somebody also trying to find somebody.

"Excuse me," a woman says as she jostles past Dante. Realizing that he's in the way, Dante threads his way to a small, empty table in the back corner and takes the chair facing the entrance. He checks the time on a wall clock. He's seventeen minutes early.

Unable to browse the Internet on his antiquated cellular telephone, Dante distracts himself by looking around the cafe. He repositions himself on his chair. He gets the urge to urinate and wonders if he has time. He looks toward the door to the men's restroom just as someone slides inside.

At the table to his immediate right, two girls talk animatedly about something that requires several OMGs. To his left, a guy wearing gigantic DJ headphones stares at his laptop, the rectangular light of the screen reflecting in the lenses of his vintage eyeglasses. Dante feels a pang of sadness at the thought of his own machines sitting in a box in a dank basement.

As the clock ticks past 7:30, Dante starts to wonder if Takei4Life is going to show.

Maybe he's at the wrong place.

Maybe he mixed up the date.

Maybe the guy found someone else to meet instead.

Maybe the guy took one look at Dante and left.

Maybe the guy will murder Dante.

Dante scratches the back of his head and checks his phone out of habit.

A tall, middle-aged man with wire-frame glasses walks through the door. He strikes Dante as familiar, but Dante can't quite place him.

But a moment later it hits him: It is Mr. Walker. Archie's father.

Dante is just about to put his head down when Mr. Walker catches his eye and offers a small wave. A bemused look settles on his face. He seems unsure whether he's going to approach Dante, but he eventually starts to make his way over, scanning the room as he does so.

"Hi, Dante." He offers his hand and they shake. "Funny seeing you here."

"Hi, Mr. Walker."

Though the place is crowded, Dante does not invite him to sit.

"So. How are things?"

"Great," Dante says. He shifts his weight in his seat.

Mr. Walker scratches the back of his head. "Ready for school to start back up?"

"I guess." Dante leans over and peers around Mr. Walker at a young, sharply dressed Asian guy who just walked through the door. But the guy steps into line without looking around. He was kind of cute, so Dante feels a tinge of disappointment. At the same time, he doesn't want Mr. Walker to bear witness to his first date.

Archie's father follow's Dante's eyes. "Waiting for someone, eh?"

Dante shrugs.

Mr. Walker scans the room again. "Me, too."

It's then that a terrible understanding dawns over them both at the same time. There's an awkward moment like when two people arrive at a door simultaneously and try to figure out who should walk through first.

Mr. Walker runs a hand over his face and sighs. "DeeThreepio?"

Dante's eyes widen. "Takei4Life?"

Mr. Walker nods.

They look away from each other.

Dante rises, his face burning with embarrassment. "Sorry—this is—I've got to go."

Archie's father gestures for him to wait. "Just to be perfectly clear, I don't want to date you. I didn't know it was you—your profile said you were older."

Dante stands. "Don't worry, I won't tell—"

"Archie already knows. I mean, not that I'm here. With you. But he knows about the whole gay thing." Mr. Walker notices confusion flash across Dante's face. "He hasn't told you guys?"

Dante shakes his head, shock clouding his thoughts as he finally understands the real reason Archie's parents divorced. He drops back into his chair.

Mr. Walker lets out a small laugh and sits down across from him. "Figures. Does he know about you?"

Dante shakes his head again.

"I know this is really, really weird, Dante, but would you actually mind staying for a moment? I'd like to get your advice on Archie."

Dante pauses and looks toward the door. It would be so easy to leave and pretend like this never happened. But he notices the pained look in Mr. Walker's eyes. He stays. "So, do you do this often?"

"What?" Mr. Walker laughs. "Go on dates with my son's friends?"

"No," Dante says, cringing. "Meet guys online. And this isn't a date."

"Sorry—just a joke. No. This is certainly not a date. Not at all." He shakes his head. "But this is the first time. Honest. And given the results, I can't say I'm inclined to try again."

Dante nods.

"You want something to drink?" Mr. Walker asks. "I'll get you something to drink."

He gets up and steps in line, leaving Dante in a daze.

Dante thinks of Archie. He searches his memory for any clues Archie might have dropped about his father. He can't think of any. Or had he just not been listening carefully enough? His parents had been divorced for a year—how could he keep this secret for so long? Why?

Sure, whenever they all got together to game, nobody really brought up personal stuff. But this seems like something Archie should have mentioned.

Mr. Walker returns, holding two steaming mugs. He sets one in front of Dante. "Hazelnut latte. Trust me. I never drank anything but black coffee until a year ago, and then I tried this. Showed me what I'd been missing all those years."

Dante holds the cup to his nose and sniffs it. It smells good. Sweet but not sugary. He takes a sip. It burns his tongue.

"Careful," Mr. Walker says, though it is too late.

Dante sets his drink down to let it cool and waits for Mr. Walker to say something.

"So, how's Archie really doing?" he finally asks.

"Fine," Dante says. "Maybe."

"Maybe?"

Dante shrugs. "I mean, I think he's having a hard time because of the move. Starting over senior year? That's not very easy."

"I know." Mr. Walker sighs. "I think that's part of the reason he won't really talk to me—has he told you about that, at least?"

Dante shakes his head, marveling at how much they're keeping from each other. How can you be friends with people for nearly six years and never open up?

Mr. Walker continues. "I feel like I've lost him. Do you know what I mean? I lost my son. Sure, I've been able to see him every other weekend. And in two days he'll be living in my house. But even when he's with me, he's not with me. That make sense?" Dante nods. "He goes straight up to his room and just does math for some reason. He'll probably just graduate and move away. I can't help but feel like I'll lose him forever. What am I supposed to do?"

Dante does not know what to say. It's a strange thing, having his friend's father ask him for advice. He shrugs. "I don't know, Mr. Walker."

"Me neither." Mr. Walker leans back in his chair. He takes a sip of his drink and then sinks into silence.

"If you don't mind my asking," Dante says, "why didn't you just wait until he graduated? To . . . you know . . . come out."

Archie's father takes another sip of his drink. "Maybe I should have. I've asked myself that question God knows how many times. And I don't have a clear reason for why I didn't, only that I couldn't." He pauses, searching for the right words. "I had a great-uncle who lived in Iowa. He lived with his sister, my great grand-mother, his entire adult life until he died. I found out decades later that he was gay." He looks into Dante's eyes. "Can you imagine that? My God—that man lived with that secret his entire life. Stuck in that room. You *couldn't* be gay in rural Iowa back then. He just couldn't. He probably would have been killed."

Dante doesn't respond but the story sinks in, works its way into his bones. He feels like crying. He takes a sip of his own drink, which has cooled to a safer temperature.

Mr. Walker continues. "But the world has changed. People can be gay now. Sure, not everyone is going to like it. And some people are still harassed or bullied or even killed because of it. But I just got to a point where I felt like I couldn't live in a tiny room any more. I had to get out. I had to stop lying to everyone." He sighs. "Don't get me wrong, I hate what it's done to Archie. I hate that he has to suffer because of me."

"I know what you mean," Dante says, thinking of his own family. "But Archie will probably come around, Mr. Walker. Just give him some time."

"I hope so, Dante." Mr. Walker smiles. "Same with your family."

As if on cue, Dante's ancient phone rings. It does not vibrate. It does not play some clever ring tone. It actually rings with a digital clatter, like a telephone from the previous millennium that it too is from. Recognizing his grandparents' number, he lets it ring.

"Whoa," Mr. Walker laughs, eyeing the phone "The nineties are calling. Literally."

"It's nobody," Dante says, ignoring it.

"Anyways," Mr. Walker says. "How about you?"

Dante shifts in his seat. "How about me what?"

"Have you told anyone?"

Dante considers the question. "My grandparents know."

"Your choice?"

"Not really."

"How'd they take it?"

"Like they found a bunch of corpses under the floorboards of my room."

"I'm sorry about that, Dante. Just give them some time. They'll come around."

"Yeah," Dante says. "I hope so. But you know what? I've felt pretty bad about it sometimes. But most of the time I actually feel better. Lighter. Like I can finally breathe."

"I know what you mean. So why haven't you told your friends yet?"

Dante shrugs.

Mr. Walker nods.

They sit quietly for a few moments, and then Mr. Walker speaks again. "Dante, let me give you some advice here: Don't spend your whole life faking who you are. The longer you live that lie, the more you'll destroy yourself. The more you'll end up hurting others."

"What about your friends?" Dante asks after a moment. "Did they care that you're gay?"

"Not the ones who matter. Sure, when I first came out, some of them were freaked out. A few stopped talking to me right away. A lot of them just gradually drifted away."

"Oh," Dante says. His phone again rings with his grandparents' number. He ignores the call but wonders why they're calling when they know—or at least, think—he's at work. "Sorry. Go on."

"Anyways," Mr. Walker continues, adjusting his glasses. "My closest friends didn't care. Heck, they knew before I even told them. And having it out there and knowing they still loved me— God, that was the best feeling ever."

Dante tries to imagine his friends' reactions. "I don't have that many friends to begin with, and if they . . ."

Mr. Walker sighs. "I hate that this world makes us feel like that. Like we're nothing. Worthless. Defective. But trust me, you will not be alone. There will *always* be people, both gay and straight, who want to be your friend, Dante, so long as you're a decent human being and so long as you're a good friend back to them— hell, even people who aren't decent human beings manage to find friends."

Dante's phone rings for a third time. He sees that it's his grandparents again. He starts to worry it's an emergency.

"Sorry," Dante says, pushing back his chair. "I have to take this."

"No problem," Mr. Walker says.

Dante makes his way to the foyer. It's still kind of loud with the heavy rain outside, but it's slightly quieter than inside the shop. He covers one ear with a hand and then presses the phone to the other. "Grandpa? Everything okay?"

There's a silence at the other end for a few beats, and then his grandpa's voice. "Get home right this minute."

"Everything all right?" Dante asks. "Is grandma okay?"

"I said get home. Right now."

"If it's an emergency I can probably leave, but I'm at work—"

"Do not lie to me anymore, boy. Your friend Mari came by looking for you. Said you weren't at work. So get home. Now."

Dante starts to speak, but his grandpa has already ended the call. A sinking feeling settles in the pit of Dante's stomach. He heads back inside the coffee shop and quickly approaches Mr. Walker.

"Sorry, but I've got to go," Dante says, pushing in his chair. "Thanks for your advice."

Mr. Walker raises his cup. "Anytime. You in trouble?"

"Yeah."

"You probably don't want to hear this, but I'm sure they love you more than you can imagine. They just want what's best for you. Your grandparents are probably right most of the time, but everybody makes mistakes. It might take a while for them to figure this one out."

Dante nods.

"Well, I really appreciate you talking to me. You're a great kid." Before Dante walks away, Mr. Walker asks, "Can you do me a favor, though?"

"Maybe."

"Try to get Archie to talk to me. That's all I want. For him to hear me out. Hear my story."

"I'll try, Mr. Walker," Dante says and then makes his way to the exit.

He stands at the threshold contemplating the gray sky. He watches the clouds flash with lightning and then drops his eyes to the street where people rush past holding umbrellas or pulling their jackets over their heads.

Dante walks into the rain.

Sam

Passing Planets

FRIDAY

Sarah shifts and ruins everything. Sam tries to reposition his body against her, but she's already out of the bed. He pauses the show playing on the television.

Looking at her phone, Sarah says, "Sorry, I have to take this."

"Who is it?" he asks.

But she's already headed up the basement stairs, laughing with someone else.

Sam sighs. He moves into her vacated spot. It is still warm and smelling of vanilla. He denies the existence of everything and anyone else.

By the time her warmth and scent have dissipated, Sarah still has not returned. Sam stares at the screen where the episode's protagonist is paused, floating helplessly through space. He had been on a mission. He succeeded, but his fighter was damaged so he had to eject. Now he drifts, hoping his crew will somehow find him amidst all that vast and infinitely expanding silence. To make matters worse, his suit is leaking oxygen. A light inside his helmet illuminates his desperate face as he drifts through a field of stars.

Sam waits a couple more minutes.

"Sarah?" He rolls onto his back. He gazes at the exposed beams of the basement ceiling, where a few glow-in-the-dark stars still stick to the rotting wood. There used to be more, there used to be a whole galaxy of constellations glowing a pale green over-head whenever it was dark enough. But over the years, the cheap adhesive had failed, and most of the plastic stars had fallen, their descent nowhere near as awe-inspiring as that of their celestial counterparts.

Sitting up, he clicks play, and the lost pilot continues to drift through the void. Sam wishes that he could give the stranded man the air in his own lungs, that he could call the crew and alert them to the emergency. But since he can't, he holds his breath in solidarity.

By the end of the episode, the crew has saved the pilot in the nick of time, just as his oxygen meter went red and he lost consciousness. Sam lets the credits roll, still in the trance of the narrative.

He hears Sarah making her way down the steps just as the TV screen goes black.

"Is it over already?" Sarah says. She drops back onto the bed next to Sam and kisses his cheek.

"Who was it?" he asks.

"Huh?"

"On the phone."

"Oh. Jenny. She wanted to know if I—if we—wanted to come to this show with her tonight. Her boyfriend's band is opening. So what do you say?"

Sam pulls the blankets around his shoulders. "Meh. I think I'd rather just stay in with you and watch a few more episodes."

Sarah rolls her eyes. "You've seen *Battlestar Galactica* like a billion times. How many chances will you get to see Jenny's boyfriend's band?"

"I hate going to those shows." Sam props up his head against the basement wall. "I'm always the only guy not wearing skinny jeans, a flannel shirt, and horn-rimmed glasses. The only guy without a beard. And there are never any seats. And everyone's always pressing up against you. It's suffocating. And I never know the words. So I always just end up standing there like an idiot while everyone else sings along. It's the worst. But this," Sam gestures to the screen, "this is genius."

"But you already know what happens."

"Yeah, but what makes the story great is that you know all of this and still you believe that there's a chance they're not going to make it," Sam says, letting his head slip back down to the bed.

With this particular episode, he pictures the crew searching some other star system while the pilot's oxygen runs out. He imagines the body, preserved by the cold vacuum of outer space, quietly passing planets, undiscovered right up until the universe ends. There's something in this scenario that calls to Sam.

"Yeah, *you*," Sara says. "Not *me*."

Sam sighs.

Sarah reaches beneath the covers and pinches Sam's butt. "Anyways. It's cool if you want to stay in and be Old Man Sam, but I'm going out on the town."

"Whatever," Sam says. "Want to make out for a little first?"

"Sorry, Samwise. Jenny wanted me to meet up with her ASAP."

"Bye, then."

"Bye."

Sam watches her go. He listens to her waning footfalls on the floor that is his ceiling.

A plastic star falls and lands on his face.

A Nice Pilipina

SATURDAY

Sam watches the steam rise off his rice. Dishes clink softly around him like white noise.

"Earth to Sam?" someone calls from somewhere. Grace elbows him in the ribs, and he emerges from his thoughts.

"Your *pather* asked you a question," Sam's mother says in her thick Filipino accent. She means *father*, not *pather*. Even after living in the United States for decades, she's retained her homeland's habit of substituting Ps for Fs.

"*Opo*. Yes, ma'am."

"Lia Santos," his father repeats. "The Santos's oldest daughter. Earned a full scholarship to Johns Hopkins. Are you friends with her?"

Sam shrugs.

His father looks around the table, a bemused smile set on the corner of his lips. "Don't you know your Filipino classmates?"

"I didn't know I had any Filipino classmates."

"Bah. That's a shame. I knew everyone in my school back in Batangas. I was class president every year." He beams at the memory while dipping a *lumpia* roll in a shallow dish containing vinegar and pepper.

Sam and Grace exchange a knowing look, having heard their father recite this fact a million times. Of course, he always forgets to mention that there were about twenty kids in his village school.

Forgoing the large bowl of *sinigang* in the middle of the table, Sam grabs a couple pieces of leftover fried chicken from a plate next to the soup. It was from three nights ago, but that's how things work at Sam's house. Food reappears at every meal until all of it has been eaten.

"How is that essay coming along, Grace?" his father asks his sister, referring to her summer assignment for her advanced English class.

"Fine," Grace mumbles without looking up from her food.

Their father grunts with approval. "Good. You need to keep getting good grades. Then you can get a full scholarship to Princeton. Or Harvard. Maybe in a few years the Santoses will be sitting around dinner talking about you!"

He laughs, as if this were some joke instead of a thinly veiled jab at Sam's academic mediocrity.

Everyone falls back into silence as they continue to eat. Sam tries to finish his meal as quickly as possible so he can return to the basement and text Sarah about hanging out later that night.

He thinks of last week, when he told Sarah a stupid joke that made her snort with laughter. He then thinks of all the times he made her laugh, and then all the times he fell asleep with his ear pressed to the phone with her at the other end, and then all of the times he held her close as she whispered into his ear.

That is what matters. Not a summer English assignment. Not grades. Not getting accepted to Harvard. Why doesn't anyone seem to get that?

"May I be excused?" Sam asks, pushing his plate away.

His mother leans forward and examines its contents. She shakes her head. "There's still meat on that chicken. And pinish your rice."

Sam does not want to finish his rice. Always rice. Every meal. He can't wait to move out and eat like a normal American. But until then, it's either eat the rice or hear his parents nag him about eating the rice. He douses his remaining portion in soy sauce and shoves a spoonful into his mouth.

"So," his mother says, "what are your plans por tonight, Sam?"

"Hanging out with Sarah," he answers after he finishes chewing. "Probably." He hadn't actually heard from her all day.

His father takes a sip from his bottle of San Miguel. "I like Sarah. But I think you're spending too much time with her. It's distracting you from your studies. Your grades have been dropping." Sam does not point out that they were never very high to begin with. "And since you have no scholarship, your mother and I think you should start working at the restaurant again so you can save up."

Sam shoves another spoonful of rice into his mouth. He really does not want to go back to work at his parents' restaurant.

His mother adds, "You can still spend some time with that girl. But maybe less. Besides, it's not serious. She is not one of us. Your cousins will pind you a nice Pilipina."

"I'm done." Sam pushes away from the table and retreats to the basement. He puts on the original *Star Trek* and spends the rest of the night exploring the final frontier while waiting to hear from Sarah.

About the Room

SUNDAY

The next night, Sam has still not heard from Sarah. Every text and e-mail he sent her has gone unanswered. So he finally decides to walk to Sarah's house, two doors down from his. There's an unfamiliar white car in the driveway. He makes a mental note to ask her about it.

He knocks several times before the door opens just a crack. Sarah slides out, quickly closing the door behind her. Her hair is up, loose strands giving her a harried look. Her cheeks are flushed. Her sleeves are rolled up.

"Hey, Samwise," she says and hugs him.

He wants to be mad at her. But she gives him a genuine Sarah-hug. Sarah-hugs are his favorite.

But after the hug ends, he lets himself be mad at her.

"Where have you been?" he asks.

Sam pulls a cigarette from his pocket, lights it, and hands it to Sarah. She blows the smoke out of the side of her mouth in the shape of a ring. The circle of smoke expands and disappears. She tucks a loose strand of hair behind her ear.

She says, "Dude, my dad's on a real cleaning kick. Been mopping and scrubbing and dusting like crazy. My God, the dusting. You ever notice how much dust there is on the top of a door? It's wild."

"It only takes like a second to send a text," Sam says.

She takes his hand. "I know. I'm sorry, Samwise." She leans into him and kisses his neck. It sends shivers down his spine. "Just lost track of time. That cleaning product must have messed with my brain."

"It's okay, I guess," he says. "I was just getting worried."

She passes him the cigarette, and he takes a drag. He tries to blow a smoke ring like Sarah did, but he fails miserably. "So you want to hang out, or what?" he asks.

"I'd love to, Samwise. But my dad told me I can't leave the house until we've cleaned every inch of it."

"How long will that take?"

She thinks about it. "Let's chill tomorrow night, okay? We'll go to the playground."

Sam likes the playground. The playground is where they fool around.

"Okay," he says.

She says goodbye and kisses him on the cheek. Then she disappears back inside her house, just as careful not to let him see inside as before.

Sam puts the cigarette between his lips and walks down her driveway. He passes the white car that he forgot to ask about.

An Infinite Number of Parallel Universes

MONDAY

"Push me," Sarah says.

Sam hops off his swing and gets behind her. He grabs the chains on either side of her seat, pulls her back as far as he can, and then runs forward. He pushes with all his might, passing beneath her feet and moving clear of her arc. She cuts through the darkness like a pendulum.

Returning to his swing, Sam gets a running start and then gets himself moving. He pumps his legs and shifts his weight until he's maximized the swing's potential. He tries to synchronize his movement with Sarah's, but they're always off. Sometimes by a little. Mostly by a lot.

"Jump!" Sarah calls and does just that at the peak of her next forward swing. Her body hangs in the air for a second before plummeting downward, hair flying out behind her. A moment later she lands expertly in the woodchips.

"Hey, you didn't jump," Sarah says, turning around.

Sam swings back and forth a few more times and then releases his grip on the chains and lets the momentum carry him off the seat. He sails into the air, and his stomach sinks as his body drops. He lands hard next to Sarah and stumbles forward, falling. He throws out his hands, smacks the ground, and immediately a sharp stab of pain shoots up from his right palm.

"Shit," he says, bringing himself back to his feet.

"You all right?" she asks. She takes his hand in hers and then turns it over.

There's a large splinter sticking into his skin just below the thumb. Blood trickles out in a surprisingly constant rivulet.

"Hold still," Sarah says. "It's deep."

"That's what she said," Sam says.

Sarah ignores him and extracts a sliver of wood the size of a toothpick. Fresh pain blossoms within his hand. He presses his palm to his mouth and sucks at the wound.

"Does it hurt?" Sarah asks.

"A little," Sam says, his saliva tasting of nicotine and blood. He wipes his palm on the leg of his jeans and then shakes his hand as if doing so will dispel the lingering pain.

"Put hydrogen peroxide on that when you get home."

"Thanks, Mom," Sam says.

Sarah holds up her hands in mock surrender. "Just trying to help."

"You know how you can help . . ." Sam says, sitting back on the swing and pulling Sarah into his lap. He presses his lips to hers. Her mouth is soft and warm. "Want to move to the tree house?" he asks, referring to the play structure that is the centerpiece of the playground. Low walls line the uppermost level of the tree house, shielding the interior from view.

"Hmm. What time is it?" Sarah asks.

"I don't know. Left my phone at home."

"Mine's in the car," she says, sliding off his lap. "Be right back."

Sam spins himself in the swing, frustrated.

Sarah returns a moment later, eyes on her phone's screen. "Shit, Samwise. It's Monday. Archie's left me like a bajillion texts about D&D. Maybe we should head back."

"It's probably too late now."

"They're going to be pissed," Sarah says.

"It won't kill them if we miss one session. They'll figure out something. They're a plucky bunch."

"I guess you're right. Anyways, I should probably get going. It's pretty late."

Sam, remaining in the swing, tries to take her hand, but she resists, still looking at her phone. He assumes she's reading through missed texts from other people. "What's going on, Sarah?" he asks.

Picking up on the worry in his voice, Sarah finally looks up. "What do you mean?"

"With us. We seem off. You seem off. Is everything all right?"

Sarah slides the phone into her back pocket. "Yeah . . . I've just got something going on right now. Family stuff."

Anticipating her need, Sam lights a new cigarette and hands it to her. "Want to talk about it?"

"Not really," she says, taking it from him.

"Oh."

"But I promise I will soon . . ."

Sam plants his feet and stops the swing from swaying. He looks down and then up into the dark sky. A bird or a bat or something flits by overhead. "Okay."

"I can't believe how long we've known each other," Sarah says, finally settling into the swing next to Sam. "I mean, damn, dude. Who would have thought when we were kids playing around here that we'd be where we are today."

"Still at the same playground?" Sam asks.

"That's not what I mean."

"I know," Sam says. "I've been rewatching old *Star Trek*. I'm at 'Mirror, Mirror.' You remember that one?"

Sarah shakes her head, unable to recall the episode.

"You know, the one where Kirk and his crew are replaced by evil doppelgangers from a parallel universe? Mirror-Spock has a goatee?"

"Oh, yeah," Sarah says, though Sam doubts she actually remembers it.

"Do you think there really are other universes out there?" he asks.

"Huh?"

Sam looks up at the sky. "Like in *Star Trek*. Somewhere in the fabric of space-time, worlds just like this one, but different variations. With other Sarahs. Other Sams. Who have goatees and stuff."

Sarah shrugs. She slides off the swing and walks over to the teeter-totter. She pushes it down and then sits on the low end, cigarette dangling from her lips.

Sam follows her. "Maybe there's one where you never moved to my block. Where we never grew up together. Never walked to school together every single day."

"That'd be a terrible universe to live in," Sarah says.

After taking the other end of the teeter-totter and lifting Sarah a foot or so, Sam says, "But I can't help but feel that's what all of the other ones must be like. That if there really are an infinite number of parallel universes out there, this is probably the only one in which we're together."

Sarah smirks. "Why do you say that?"

"It's just . . ." Sam hesitates. "I'm not delusional. I know I was lucky that you moved in two doors down from me. If you lived on the other side of town, there's no way we would have ever dated."

"Why do you think that?"

"Just look at who you hang out with."

"Archie? Dante? Mari? They're your friends, too."

Sam shakes his head. "It's not like you hang out with them outside of our gaming nights."

"Okay. I'll give you that."

"I'm talking about the kids you sit with at lunch. The ones you always go to shows in the city with. Jenny. Ryan. Chad. The others whose names I don't even know. Honestly, I think I just hold you back."

"I've been happy with you, Samwise."

Sarah's use of the present perfect tense strikes Sam as ironic.

"I've always expected my luck won't last," he says. "I've always kind of felt like a plane flying with one engine out, waiting for the other to fail. Just waiting to fall out of the sky. Crash into the ocean. Sink to the bottom of the sea."

Sarah steps off the teeter-totter and Sam's end lowers to the ground. She drops the butt of the cigarette and steps on it.

"Let's go home," she says. "This is depressing as hell."

That night, Sam dreams that he is in an elevator. The interior is wire-brushed stainless steel, so he sees only a vague blur in place of his reflection. He is not naked and he is glad about this, because he senses that people are often naked in such dreams.

But there are no buttons at the sides of the doors and no display at the top to indicate the passing floors. There is not even that pleasant Muzak for which elevators are so infamous. There is only the sense that the elevator is descending. Sam waits, eager to see where it will stop, what the doors will slide open to reveal. Several minutes pass and Sam still feels his stomach dropping as the elevator continues to plummet to some unknown level.

Finally, after what feels like an eternity, he feels the elevator slow and then come to rest.

The doors slide open.

In front of him is an expanse of nothingness. Vast and blank. Cold and lonely. Space without the stars.

Not to Be Deterred

TUESDAY

Sam knows he is losing Sarah. He senses it as clearly as he does the shifting of the seasons.

Only, he does not know why.

Hasn't he been a good boyfriend? He has always been there for her. When her dad lost his job and things got tough around her house. When her mom moved out. Sam was always there for Sarah. To listen. To console. To cheer up.

Time and time again, he places her happiness above all else, even his own.

So why is she pulling away?

He repositions himself within his cocoon of covers. *The Last Man on Earth* is playing on TV, but he's not paying any attention to it. Upstairs, he hears his mom singing along with a karaoke machine, her voice straining to hit a high note.

In an astronomically rare moment, Sam decides that he needs some fresh air. He grabs a pair of jeans and a hoodie from the floor. He sniffs them, decides they are acceptable, and pulls them on. He heads upstairs, slips past his mom unnoticed, and steps outside.

The world is light and noise. The sun shines bright in the clear sky. Kids are outside riding bikes and bouncing balls, reveling in the last days of summer. Sam puts up his hood and pulls the brim down over his eyes to block the sun. He starts walking away from the lively scene.

After ten or fifteen minutes, Sam passes the last house on the last street in his subdivision. He continues along the sidewalk as it dips into a small patch of trees, the developer's sad attempt at a nature trail. Still, it is more peaceful, even if it is just a few feet beyond the reach of humanity. Leaves rustle like overhead waves. Birds chirp.

Sam walks slowly, his hands tucked into the pockets of his hoodie.

Maybe it's because he's not trying hard enough.

Maybe he should try to listen to more of the music she likes. Watch the primetime television shows she prefers. Talk to the friends she sits with at lunch.

Sam sighs. It all sounds so exhausting.

Yet he knows he must do something before it's too late. Or he will lose her. And if he loses her, then who will love him?

Walking under trees, noting that their leaves will fall within the month, Sam tries to recall every romantic comedy Sarah ever made him watch. He compiles a mental list of every sweeping romantic gesture John Cusack or Hugh Grant or Ryan Reynolds or whatever hapless white guy did to win back the loves of their lives.

In the end, he decides upon three manageable courses of action, confident that at least one will work. He turns around and starts walking back up the path. After a few minutes, it rejoins the street and the subdivision. A group of middle school boys bike past him, popping wheelies.

"Loser!" one of them shouts.

Sam ignores the provocation. He keeps walking until he arrives home and then slips into the basement like a fish returning to the deep.

He makes his way over to a neglected corner that is piled with boxes and junk and begins rooting through the years. Just as he's about to give up, he finds his old piano keyboard at the bottom of a box that's filled with musty stuffed animals. He pulls it out with some effort and carries it over to his bed. He dusts off the keyboard using a shirt he picks up from the floor.

Sam sits down cross-legged on his bed and sets the keyboard in his lap. He places his fingers over the keys and pauses like he's trying to resurrect the dead. No clear memories emerge, and, for the first time in his life, he wishes that he had not thrown that one fit in the third grade that resulted in his father allowing him to quit piano lessons.

Not to be deterred by a mere lack of skill, Sam presses the power button. The keyboard comes to life.

He starts pressing random keys. The sounds he makes are horrible, discordant. His playing does not improve over time. Sam cannot even recall the major and minor chords. Giving up on his first idea—writing Sarah a song—he sets aside the keyboard and makes his way upstairs to try to carry out his second.

"Can I borrow some money, *Nanay*?" he asks his mom.

She stops singing and lowers the karaoke mic. On the television screen, the words to a song continue to light up in rhythmic sequence as the instrumental track plays on. A montage of random tropical scenes shows in the background. "What hab you done to earn it?" she asks, her accent confusing V with B.

Sam scratches the back of his head. "Um."

"You go back to work in the restaurant," she says, "and you will hab money."

His mom goes back to her song, and with that, Sam's second idea—buying Sarah a meaningful present—dies a sudden death.

He was hoping it would not come to the third option. It requires so much more work. But it is the only way.

Sam sighs and returns to the basement. He decides that today is an unlucky day, so, instead, he will win back her love tomorrow.

The Adoring Gaze of Rekindled Romance

WEDNESDAY

Sam waits until dark and then grabs his backpack and heads to Sarah's house. But he does not knock on the door. Instead, he climbs on to the porch railing where it meets the side of the house, trying to make as little noise as possible.

Once he's standing on top of the railing, he slips off his backpack and swings it onto the portion of the roof that hangs over the porch and under Sarah's window. He listens for a moment to see if it will roll back down, but it stays. Reaching up, he grips the edge of the roof with both hands. He counts to three in his head and hops, pulling himself up the rest of the way. It is neither easy nor elegant nor noiseless. But with considerable effort, he manages.

Leaning over, he grabs the backpack and then scoots up and over until he is out of the square of muted light that spills from her room. He leans his back against the side of the house.

Sam exhales, taking a moment to rest and appreciate his accomplishment so far. He brushes off the gravel bits from the shingles that have stuck to his palms and then shakes off the hand he injured the other night. He looks out over the neighborhood. A few streetlights are blinking to life.

He notices that the white car is back in Sarah's driveway. It is not hers. It is not her dad's. Maybe she has a relative in town.

Sam's attention shifts when he hears music start playing inside Sarah's room. Though it is muffled by the walls, he can make out the melody and the sound of male and female voices rising and falling in harmony. It sounds familiar, but Sam cannot recall the name of the song or of the band.

He listens for a moment longer. Wonders what Sarah might be doing at that very moment. Probably just lying back on her bed with her phone in hand, checking her social networks.

He eases closer to the window and starts to lean over for a peak—but then stops. If she sees him now, that will ruin everything. First, he must set up.

Unzipping the backpack, he takes out the flannel blanket. He shakes it out and then lays it down on the roof. Next, he pulls out a couple bottles of alcoholic lemonade that he stole from the fridge. He sets them down, not pulling his hands away until he's certain that they won't slide down the gradual slope. Then he removes paper plates, plastic silverware, and a couple of containers with food that he heated up just before leaving his house.

After he finishes arranging the rooftop picnic, he pulls out one final item from his backpack: a fat, temporary paint marker used to write on car windows. He scoots over to the window and begins writing, trying to make as little noise as possible.

I, he draws, a foot tall, across the top of her window.

L-O-V-E, he draws across the middle.

He starts to write the final line across the bottom of the window. But before he finishes the *O*, the curtain pulls back. Sarah peers through the window at Sam, an expression of utter confusion on her face. It is not the adoring gaze of rekindled romance he was hoping for.

She pulls open the window and sticks her head outside. "Sam? What the hell are you doing out here?"

"Um," he says.

"Why are you writing on my window? What's all that stuff?"

He realizes for the first time that, from her perspective, his message was backwards, his actions perhaps pervy. "Oh, um, I wanted to—"

He stops speaking as he beholds the inside of her room.

It takes him a moment to register what he is seeing. He blinks. Rubs his eyes. But it's still the same.

Bare walls. Stacks of boxes. Missing furniture.

He blinks again. "You're moving."

"Shit," she says, "I didn't want you to find out like this."

"Where?"

"Seattle—my dad got a new job with—"

"When?"

". . . Tomorrow. Morning."

Without saying anything, Sam tosses the marker over the house. He starts to gather everything and stuffs it all into his backpack as quickly as possible.

"Look, Sam, calm down. Come inside so we can talk about this, please."

He zips up his bag, climbs back down, and walks away.

"Sam," she calls after him, but he keeps walking. Down her driveway. Past his house. Past his neighborhood.

He does not stop walking until he reaches the playground. He finds a trash can, stuffs the backpack inside, and crawls inside a tunnel slide.

Indentations

THURSDAY

"Mommy, there's someone in here."

Sam slowly stirs. He is uncomfortably warm because the morning sun has heated the inside of the tube. Opening his eyes, he looks up the slide and sees a child peering down at him from the top.

"Sorry," Sam says. He crawls out the bottom of the slide and stretches his sore limbs. A woman—probably the kid's mom—is staring at him, phone in hand. Sam waves to indicate that he is not planning to abduct her child, and then starts for home.

As he reaches his street, he spots the moving truck in Sarah's driveway. A couple of men—who look exactly like how he imagined moving men would—are lifting a bookshelf into the back of the truck.

Sam walks into his house, glad to find it empty. He does not feel like explaining to anyone what is going on, where he has been. As if they would ask. The only texts he received last night were from Sarah who wanted him to come back so they could talk, and from Dante wondering where he was. Sam's parents probably didn't even notice that he was out all night.

Returning to the basement, Sam can't shake the terrible feeling that settled into his stomach the moment he saw Sarah's packed up room. It stirs within him like something alive. He imagines it as a malevolent creature, covered in bristly hair and spikes, amoebic and expanding.

He slides underneath his blankets and tries to go back to sleep. But he can't. The creature won't let him.

He sighs a pathetic sigh and wonders if it's even possible to sigh nonpathetically. He gives it a few tries and concludes that it is not. He sighs, pathetically, once more and climbs out of bed. He goes to the small ground-level window on the side of the basement that faces Sarah's house.

Sam observes the moving men work for about ten minutes. His patience is rewarded when he sees Sarah emerge. She walks out of the garage, head down and thumbs hooked into the belt loops of her jeans. She steps across her lawn, approaching Sam's house.

Sam panics—He has not showered. He hasn't brushed his teeth. He's still wearing the same thing as last night. He strips and puts on a different set of crumpled clothes that he gathers up from the floor.

Sam waits at the bottom of the stairs for Sarah's knock. He does not want to appear too pathetic. He does want to look like the visual form of the sighs he had been practicing earlier.

But the house remains silent.

Sam continues to wait, allowing time for a shoe she might have stopped to tie. He moves back to the window. Sarah is nowhere in sight. He stands on his tiptoes and presses his face to the dingy glass in an attempt to gain a new angle. But still no Sarah.

Sam climbs the stairs but finds only one of his shoes next to the door. He returns to the basement to search for the other one, but he does not have time to look for it. So he opts to cover his other foot with one of his mom's bamboo house slippers and steps outside.

The sky is overcast. The wind carries the scent of rain. A lawn mower drones in the distance. The hollow stomping of the mover's boots upon the inside of the truck resounds through the neighborhood.

It feels like his hair is sticking up in back. He tries to smooth it down with his hands. It doesn't work.

As he approaches Sarah's driveway, he peers inside the truck. It's nearly full.

"Out the way, kid!" a mover calls to Sam while backing out of the garage.

He's carrying one end of a beige couch. His partner emerges a moment later with the other end. Sam catches a whiff of body odor and sawdust.

He steps aside and recalls the nights he had spent on that couch with Sarah, sharing a blanket and watching movies. It feels wrong that the movers' hands are on it now. It feels as if they are groping not just the couch but Sam and Sarah. He hates the movers in that moment, even though he knows his hatred is illogical. He looks at their stupid moving belts and stupid gloves without fingertips and thinks of how stupid the movers are. He wants to yell at them to be more careful. To be less stupid.

Whatever.

Sam slips past them, through the garage, and into the house.

Given the contents of the truck, Sam knows the rooms will be nearly empty. But the barren quality still shocks him. It's just so alien. On his way to Sarah's room at the end of the hallway, he peeks through the passing doorways. Nothing remains. This is real. He continues up the stairs.

He finds Sarah's door slightly ajar. He takes a moment to return the blank stare of the bare wood and then enters.

The room Sam had known was dark and chaotic. Band posters, advertisements for concerts, and album covers had covered every inch of the walls and even some of the ceiling. Clothing, sneakers, and books had littered nearly every inch of the floor. On one side of her room had been her bed, sheets perpetually in disarray. White Christmas lights—which Sarah referred to as "party lights" when out of season—had lined the ceiling. And during the day there was always a red glow cast by the sunlight shining through her red curtains.

Now, her room is nothing but light and air. For the first time in years, Sam looks at the actual walls. They are lavender. He looks at the carpet. It is beige. He looks out a window. There is a pine tree.

Sam feels as if he is a space traveler, marveling at a barren planet that was once some great civilization.

"Sarah?" he calls. The word echoes.

"In here." Sarah's voice drifts out of the closet, small and distant.

The sound anchors this moment in reality. It is actually happening. Unlike Archie, Sarah isn't moving across the river but across the country. Sam sighs.

He follows her voice and wonders once again at the transformation. Without clothes crammed on the racks and junk piled on the floor, it is apparently a small walk-in closet. Sarah sits on the floor with her back against a wall.

"Hi," she says.

"Hi," Sam says.

She sniffs and wipes her nose with the back of her sleeve.

Sam sits on the closet floor against the wall opposite her.

"Hi," Sam says again.

"Hi."

"So you're all packed?"

"Mostly," she says. "I ended up just throwing a lot of stuff away. But I saved something for you." Sarah gets up, slips out of the closet. She returns a few seconds later holding a record. She hands it to Sam and then sits down next to him.

He examines the cover, puzzled. "Thanks . . . but I don't have a record player."

"Really? You don't know why I'm giving you this?"

"Um."

"That's the album that was playing when we first kissed. Back in seventh grade." She cocks her head, an unhappy smile on her face. "You honestly don't remember?"

"I'd have to hear it," he says, though in reality he has absolutely no recollection that music was even playing. He does, however, remember that a Christmas decoration on the roof glowed through the window. That her parents were downstairs watching a movie. That her lip balm tasted like green apple.

"If you don't want it . . ." she says, reaching for the album.

Sam pulls it away. "No, I do." He examines the cover and then sets it down on the floor next to him.

She looks at Sam for a bit and then relents. "I wish you would have come inside last night. That was kind of a dick move leaving like that and then not responding to my texts."

"A dick move was not telling me you were moving. What was the plan, just to call me from Seattle?"

A long minute passes in silence. Neither wants to fight. Between them is a confused mess of everything they are feeling and everything they want to say but are not saying and everything they do not want to say but should say.

Sam feels a lump forming in his throat. Sadness threatens to overtake his anger.

"I can't believe you're moving," he finally says. "To the other side of the continent."

"I know," she says.

"I can't believe that the next time I hear the doorbell, I'll know it's not you."

"I know."

"I can't believe our D&D group is losing its rogue."

"I know."

"I can't believe I'll be alone. . . actually, I take that back. It's totally believable."

"Stop saying stuff like that."

"By the way," Sam says, "whose white car is that in the driveway?"

"My dad's," she says. "He bought a new one for the trip."

"Oh."

They settle back into silence.

Sam gets up, walks out of the closet, still stunned by this emptiness, by this loss. Tiny square indentations are pressed into the carpet, left behind by the furniture. Using these as cues, he tries to reconstruct the room in his mind.

That is where her bed goes.

That is where her desk goes. Her computer. Her record player.

That is where her bookshelf goes. Her lamp. Her nightstand.

Her.

But his memory falters, and the imagined shadows fade back to emptiness.

Sarah comes up to Sam and stands next to him, trying to see what he sees.

"Your room feels so much bigger now that it's empty." Sam's eyes stay on the floor.

"I know, right? But it's been great for practicing my cartwheels," says Sarah. Then she does a cartwheel, ending with her hair over her face and hands raised in triumph.

"Yeah, I don't know. It still looks pretty sloppy to me."

Sarah feigns offense and punches Sam in the arm.

He laughs as he takes the hit.

"Then you do one," she challenges.

"No way."

"Why not?"

"I'm training for the national cartwheel championships and my coach doesn't want me to publicly cartwheel. You know, in case of spies."

"God, you're such a dork," Sarah says and smiles.

"Sorry. It's just a really competitive sport."

Sarah smiles again. Sam returns to the closet and sits on the floor. He hugs his legs to his chest and buries his face in his knees.

Sarah sits down next to Sam. She puts her arm around him and leans her head onto his shoulder. Sam tries to memorize the feel of their bodies pressed against one another.

He takes a deep breath. "So what does this mean for us?"

She covers her face with her hands. "I'm sorry, Sam, but I don't think I can do the distance thing."

Sam's stomach clenches. His eyes well up. "We don't have to break up, Sarah. What difference does physical distance make anymore? We can still talk on the phone. We can text, e-mail, video chat. I mean, this isn't like the pioneer days where we have to wait months for the Pony Express to deliver letters. There are even airplanes now. No more caulking wagons and floating. We'll be apart, but we can still be together."

Sarah uncovers her face and looks at her shoes. "It's not as easy as that. We won't be able to hug or kiss or make out or fool around. Do you really think we'd able to stay close? I know those physical things aren't everything, but I think I need them. Like the string on a balloon."

"It's only one year. Then we can go to the same college" Sam says.

"Sam, I'll be meeting new people. Starting a completely different life. I don't know who I'll be this time next year. I don't know where I'll want to go to college."

Sam stares at his hands. He imagines himself as a red balloon released, rising into the atmosphere. "Why didn't you tell me earlier?"

"I'm sorry, Sam," she says. "I didn't want to ruin our final summer."

Sarah's father suddenly appears in the doorway of the closet.

"Time to go," he tells Sarah. "We've got a long drive ahead of us."

"Okay. Be right down," Sarah says.

"And, Sam, if you're ever in Seattle, you're more than welcome to stay with us."

"Thanks, Mr. Hall," Sam says.

Mr. Hall leaves.

Sam and Sarah stand.

They wrap their arms around each other. They stay like that for a while, but not long enough for Sam.

"I'll always love you, Sam," she says.

"This proves otherwise," he says.

The Party, Gathered

Colossally Stupid

FRIDAY, 11:53 P.M.

Sam closes the door and then pauses for a moment, holding his breath. He listens until he is certain that he did not wake his family, and then he turns his back to his house. He wishes that he would have said goodbye to Grace. He has no way of knowing when he'll see her again.

Street lights illuminate patches of the sidewalk as he passes his neighbors' houses, their windows all dark. He wonders about each of them. He wonders if they are sleeping, and if they are sleeping, what they are dreaming. A dog barks somewhere in the distance. And then another dog barks somewhere else.

He rounds the corner and spots the car. Its headlights flash twice. He nods.

As Sam approaches, he sees Mari behind the wheel, Dante in the front, and Archie in the back. Sam waves as he passes in front of the headlights, and the trunk pops open. He drops his bags inside and then climbs into the back seat next to Archie.

"The band is back together," Archie says, patting Sam on the back.

Nobody laughs.

"Thanks again, guys," Sam says, as Mari pulls away from the curb. "It means a lot that you'd come with me."

"It beats moving in with my father," Archie says.

"Or working at McCluck's," Dante says.

"Or my mom bugging me about . . ." Mari starts, but doesn't finish. "Anyways, everyone knows this is colossally stupid, right?" Nobody responds. "And you all know we're going to get in major trouble?"

"By the time they find out, we'll be long gone," says Sam.

Archie double-checks his seatbelt. "We've never gotten in any real trouble before, so how mad can our parents get?"

Dante takes a deep breath.

"Just think of it like a quest," Archie continues. "But in real life. We need the experience points."

Mari shifts the car into gear. "Seattle, here we come."

Through the Night

SATURDAY, 3:01 A.M.

Archie examines his cheek in the dirty mirror. The rest stop bathroom's pallid lighting doesn't reveal much. "I think my beard's finally coming in."

Dante chuckles as he flushes and then joins Archie at the sinks. He waves his hand under the automatic sensor, but nothing happens. He tries the next one, but again nothing.

"You can use this one," Archie says, moving over. "I'm done."

"Thanks."

"So I'm surprised you came along, big guy," Archie says. "They let you take off work like that?"

Dante shrugs. "Hey, Arch, can I ask you something about your dad?"

Archie punches the large metallic button, and the roar of the hand dryer drowns out Dante. He walks out before the machine stops. He agreed to come to get *away* from his dad.

And to spend time with Mari. He just hoped she'd forgive him for last night. Whatever it was he had done wrong.

Archie surveys the parking lot on his way back to the car. There are only a few vehicles, most of which seem as if they're settled in for the night. A middle-aged woman examines her choices in the outdoor vending machines. A lamp flickers overhead.

"I don't know if anyone's told you," Archie says, arriving at the car where Sam leans against the hood smoking, "but those things'll kill you."

Sam responds by trying to exhale a ring of smoke but fails. He coughs. "Want one? You won't look as nerdy anymore."

"No, thanks," Archie says, joining Sam on the hood. He looks toward the restrooms while waiting for Mari to appear. "So you actually think this will work? You think you'll get Sarah back?"

"Maybe," Sam says. "She said it was because she couldn't do distance."

"So, what? You planning on living there?"

Sam takes a drag from his cigarette. "Maybe. I'm eighteen."

"What if that's not the real reason she dumped you?" Archie asks.

"What do you mean?" Sam says.

"I mean, what if she didn't break up with you because she's moving, but because she just didn't want to date you anymore?"

"Fuck you," Sam says.

"No offense," Archie says, holding up his hands defensively. "But for real, I'm just trying to think through this logically. I think sometimes people are too afraid to do what they know they need to do. They wait for something to let them off the hook. Maybe for her, moving provided a convenient excuse."

"Like I said: Fuck you."

Archie shrugs. "Whether you get her back or not, you owe us."

"Why? You chose to come. Everyone did."

Archie can't really argue with that. He lifts his eyes to the night sky. It must be overcast because there are neither stars nor a moon.

A few moments later, Dante returns, followed by Mari. The four stand in a circle, each waiting for someone else to say something.

Sam puts out his cigarette against the rusty hood of Mari's car and then flicks away the butt. She glares at him, but he ignores it.

"We're making pretty good time," he says. "Already halfway across Pennsylvania. Should make it late Sunday or early Monday if we drive straight through the night."

"Well, I need to rest," Mari says. "So you want to drive next?" She holds out the keys.

"No, thanks," Sam says.

"It's your freaking girlfriend we're going to see," Mari says.

"*Ex*," Archie says. "His *ex*-girlfriend."

Sam ignores Archie. "I'm paying for all the gas."

"Yeah, with your dad's credit card," says Archie.

Sam turns to him. "What are you contributing, Arch?"

"My delightful presence." He smiles.

"You should help drive."

"Never got my license, remember?"

Sam lets out a sarcastic laugh. "Oh, yeah. Mommy and Daddy drive you everywhere."

"Here." Dante holds out his hand for the keys. "Let's just go."

Mari drops them into his palm. "Yes, please."

Archie flashes a victorious smile at Sam.

Onward to Discover

SATURDAY, 6:58 A.M.

Mari wakes at the sudden jarring sound of the tires hitting the rumble strip. She feels the car slowing, and when she opens her eyes, Dante is pulling over onto the shoulder. Other cars continue rushing past.

"Why are we stopping?" she asks. "We get pulled over?"

Sam and Archie, also awake now, look through the back window. There is no cop car, only the unrelenting flow of traffic. The sun has just barely risen, hanging just above the highway behind them.

"Look," Dante says. He kills the engine and tilts his chin toward a white, rectangular sign about thirty or forty feet in front of them.

Welcome to Ohio, it says. *So Much to Discover!*

"I thought it'd be bigger," Mari says.

"That's what she said," Archie says.

He looks to see if she smiles. She does not.

"Why are we wasting time?" Sam asks, his mouth sour from sleep.

"If we turn around now," Dante says, "we can be back home in time to say that we went out together for a late breakfast or lunch or something. None of us would get in trouble."

"Is that what you want?" Mari asks.

"We're wasting time," says Sam. "Keep driving."

"I'm already in trouble, so it doesn't make much difference to me," Dante says.

"For what?" Archie asks. A semi-truck whizzes by in the right lane, causing their car to sway. Dante just shakes his head.

"Out with it, big guy," Archie says.

"It doesn't matter," he says. "I just want to make sure everyone's okay with doing this."

"Yes. Now let's go," Sam says.

Archie removes his glasses, fogs the lenses with his breath, and then wipes them with his shirt. "Well, everyone knows I'm more than happy to peace out for a few days."

Dante notices Mari hasn't said anything. "Mari?"

She looks out the window at the trees. She thinks. About their leaves. About the unread letter pressed into her notebook. About a tumor lurking within her mother. About Archie. "I'm cool with it. Need some inspiration. I've come down with a little case of writer's block."

Sam says, "Let's go."

"Wait," Dante says. "Everyone should call home first. Tell them where we've gone."

"That's fucking stupid," Sam says. "You're getting into trouble wrong."

"No, Dante's right," Archie says. "What do you think your parents will do when they can't find you?"

"They won't even notice I'm gone," Sam says.

"Fine," Archie says. "But what do you think my parents will do? Or Mari's? Or Dante's grandparents?"

Sam relents. "They'll call."

"And if we don't answer? If we don't notify them of our impromptu cross-country journey?" Archie asks.

"Then they'll call the police and report you missing," Sam mumbles.

Archie pats Sam on the head. "If I had a gold star, it'd be all yours, buddy."

Sam pulls out his phone. "I'll just text."

The others grab their phones, take a collective deep breath, and call.

"... yes, Mom, I'm fine."

"... going to Seattle ..."

"... because Sam needs to ..."

"... we're his friends ..."

"... should be back in a few days ..."

"... I know ..."

"... I'm sorry ..."

"... no ..."

"... not going to turn around ..."

"... I know ..."

"... sorry ..."

"... it won't hurt my GPA ..."

"... not learning anything real yet ..."

"... call every day ..."

"... fine ..."

"... how about one month ..."

"... that's fair ..."

"... yeah, okay ..."

"... I love you, too ..."

"... love you ..."

"... I'm sorry ..."

The calls end at nearly the same time, like rain stopping all at once. Mari, Archie, and Dante hang their heads, contrite but relieved, ready but disbelieving.

"You guys should have texted," Sam says. His phone starts to vibrate with a call. He turns it off.

"Maybe we should change seats. Sam can move up front, and Mari can come back here with me," Archie says.

Dante looks at Mari.

"I'm good," she says, stretching out her legs.

Dante restarts the engine. He waits for an opening in the traffic and then pulls back onto the highway, onward to discover.

What You Think Matters

SATURDAY, 9:43 A.M.

Archie squints, gripping the steering wheel like it might fly away. He guides the car past hilly farmland dotted with grazing cows beneath clouds that stretch across the sky like cotton pulled thin. Country music plays on the radio. He'd change the station, but it's *all* country.

Also, he's afraid to take even one hand off the wheel.

"Why do I keep swerving?" he asks.

"You're trying too hard. Just relax. Keep your eyes fixed on where you want to go, not where you are," Mari advises from the passenger seat. "And keep your speed up."

Archie relaxes a bit too much and drifts into the adjacent lane. A driver blares his car horn as he accelerates past them.

"You'll get the hang of it," Dante says, crammed into the seat behind Mari.

"Is the engine supposed to be making that sound?" Archie asks. "It's like a gerbil suffering a slow, painful death."

Mari laughs and slaps him on the shoulder. "It's always made that sound. My car's a plucky heroine."

"The road bends up ahead—what do I do?" Archie asks.

"Use the Force," Dante says.

Mari answers Archie in a soothing voice. "Just turn the car with the road. Be gentle. Remember: look where you want to go."

"Okay. All right. I think I'm getting this." He smiles.

Another car honks as it overtakes them.

"What's that in the road?" Archie asks.

Everyone looks. "Roadkill," says Sam.

"What do I do? Should I stop?"

"Just drive around it," Mari says.

"I can't—it's right in the middle," Archie says, his voice rising with panic as they close the distance.

"Then just drive over it," Sam says.

Archie glances at Sam and then back at the road. "And kill it?!"

"It's already dead."

"Yeah, but still, it seems like—Oh, God! It's right there—what do I—"

There's a *thump-thump* as the tires drive over the creature's carcass. Archie shudders and then checks his rearview mirror. "You think it's okay?"

Sam shakes his head. Dante laughs. Mari pats Archie on the shoulder again.

"Maybe someone else should take over," Sam says. "He's going like ten miles an hour. We'll be lucky to make it to Seattle by Christmas at this rate. Assuming we don't die in a fiery crash."

"There's no way we're going to make it twenty-something more hours *and* back with just Dante and me driving," says Mari. "So unless you want to put down that phone and take the wheel, I suggest you shut up and enjoy the ride."

Sam sneers at Mari and then drops his eyes back to his phone.

"Still can't get ahold of her?" Dante asks.

"No," says Sam. "Maybe she forgot her phone somewhere. She's lost it before. Plenty of times."

Archie takes his eyes off the road for an instant and exchanges a look with Mari. The car vibrates as it drifts over the rumble strip and then vibrates again as it swerves back onto the road.

"Aquaman," says Dante.

Sam thinks for a moment and then says, "Nick Fury."

"Nope," says Archie, both hands still gripping the wheel, though not as tightly as before. "Mari already used him."

"Who fucking cares?" Sam replies. "There's only so many superhero names that begin with *N*, but every other one ends with it."

"Those are the rules," says Archie.

There's a tense silence for a few miles. But just when it seems like the game has died, Sam mumbles, "Naruto."

Archie nods his approval. "Omega Red."

"Doctor Manhattan," says Mari.

"See?" Sam says.

"Nite Owl," says Dante, staying with *Watchmen*.

"L . . ." says Sam. He rolls down the window and sticks out his head. The air is warm and humid and smells of manure. The wind is loud and kicks up everyone's hair. Sam brings his head back into the car and rolls up the window. "Loki."

"Did we already use Ironman?" Archie asks. Everyone nods. Archie changes lanes and actually overtakes another car. "Invisible Woman, then."

"N again?" Mari says.

"I'll give you a hint," Archie says.

"You can't do that," Sam says.

"It's not against the rules," says Archie.

"What fucking rules? There's not like an official Superhero Alphabet Name Game rulebook. You just keep making up shit as you go."

Archie ignores Sam. "Think blue. And teleportation. Though, somewhat limited."

"Oh, Nightcrawler." She high-fives Archie. He smiles.

"Rogue," says Dante, without skipping a beat.

Sam offers, "Earthworm Jim."

"Mrs. Marvel," says Archie.

"It's technically *Ms.* Marvel," Mari says.

"You lose," Sam says.

"No, I don't. It's *Mrs.* Isn't she married? To Captain Marvel?"

"I don't think so. Anyways, trust me. It's *Ms.* She was created to attract feminist fans," Mari says.

"Shouldn't she be wearing more clothes then?" Archie asks. Before Mari can reply, Archie spots a woman in the distance, holding up a thumb while walking along the shoulder. "Speaking of feminists . . ."

"Why are you slowing down?" Sam asks, peering between the seats at the speedometer's dropping needle.

"Because I'm picking her up"

"Why?" asks Sam.

"I'm driving. I have the power."

"You sound like a super villain," Dante says.

Mari sits up. "We can't pick up a hitchhiker. What if she's a murderer?"

Sam groans. "We don't have time for this."

"Calm down, my little Asian buddy," says Archie, clicking on the turn signal. "We're on an adventure."

"Then let's stick to the main quest," Sam says.

Everyone looks at the woman as Archie pulls over and rolls the car past her.

"She looks like a hippie," Sam adds.

The car comes to a stop. Archie says, "Marigold, be a dear and roll down your window, please."

Looking into the side mirror, Mari watches the woman approach. She's white, maybe in her twenties or thirties. Skinny. Hair in dreadlocks. Pretty. Mari sighs and then does as Archie asked.

A moment later, the woman is standing outside Mari's window.

"Thanks for stopping," she says, leaning down and smiling.

Archie smiles back. "Where you headed?"

"Just up ahead to Chicago. If you're going that far. If not, as close as you can get me would be great."

Archie nods. "We're driving right past the Windy City, so it shouldn't be a problem. Right, guys?" His inquiry is met with silence, so he answers himself. "Right."

He pops the trunk and she crams her pack inside.

Reluctantly, Sam opens the door and scoots to the middle.

"Thanks again," she says as she climbs in and pulls the door shut. Her musky odor fills the car. Everyone acts like they don't notice. "My name's Sunshine, by the way."

"Of course it is," Sam says under his breath.

"It's really no problem," Archie says, returning her perpetual smile. "I'm Archie."

"Mari," Mari says, turning in her seat to shake hands with Sunshine.

Dante waves from the other side of Sam. "Dante."

Sunshine waves back.

The only one who doesn't introduce himself is Sam. After a minute, Archie says, "Sam's the grumpy little Filipino next to you. Don't worry, he doesn't bite. He's just sad."

Sunshine's face turns sympathetic. "Aww, why are you sad, Sam?"

Sam shrugs.

There's a break in traffic, and Archie pulls back onto the highway.

"This is beautiful," Sunshine says, waving her hands to indicate the car's interior.

"Really?" asks Mari. "It's kind of a piece. When my dad bought it for me it already had nearly 150,000 miles on it. Overheats all the time."

"No," Sunshine says. "I meant you guys. You're so multicultural. It's like a microcosm of America."

"We just need an Indian chief and a cop," Archie says. Sunshine laughs. But nobody else does.

"So where you all going?" she asks.

"Seattle," Sam mutters.

She nods, impressed. "That's quite the trip. What's in Seattle?"

"Sam's girlfriend," Dante says.

"*Ex*-girlfriend," Archie corrects.

"Ah, I see. That's why he's sad. On a mission to woo her back?"

"Something like that," Sam says.

"She must be some girl to inspire such a trip."

"She is," Sam says. "The best."

Sunshine nudges him with her shoulder. "That's so cute. You know how to woo her back right?"

"How?" says Sam.

"The clitoris."

Sam, Dante, and Mari turn to see if she's serious.

Archie glances at her in the rearview mirror. "Elaborate, please."

Sunshine laughs. "Wait, how old are you guys?"

"Old enough," Archie says. Mari rolls her eyes.

"Still in school?"

"Yes," Mari answers. "*High* school."

"Seniors," Archie clarifies.

"Aww," Sunshine says. She leans forward and tousles Archie's hair. He blushes. "You guys are just babies. Is this like your first road trip?"

"Kind of," Archie says.

"That's awesome. It's so cool that you guys are just hitting the road like this. I'm surprised your parents let you."

"Not so much," Mari says.

"That's even more awesome," Sunshine says and then laughs again. "If you don't mind my asking, how are you paying for everything?"

Archie navigates a bend in the highway like he's been driving for years instead of hours. "Sam stole his dad's credit card, so that's covering our gas. Everybody else chipped in what they could. I ran the numbers, and we should be able to make it back home with a few bucks to spare."

"Well, I have friends in Minnesota," Sunshine says. "Their place is close to the highway. If you make it that far tonight, I'm sure they'd let you stay with them. That way you wouldn't have to pay for a hotel. I'm sure they'd even hook you up with some food, too."

"We're not stopping," Sam says.

"Just offering is all. You little dudes are like my heroes. I didn't have the balls to just take off like this when I was in high school."

"Yeah," Archie says, readjusting his glasses. "We're veritable bad-asses."

"Well, I was Little Miss Goody-Goody when I was in high school."

"And then?" Archie asks.

"Life," Sunshine says. "The Road."

"What the hell does that even mean?" Sam asks while looking out the window.

"You'll understand by the time you get to Seattle."

"Isn't hitchhiking dangerous?" Dante asks.

Sunshine reaches into a pocket and pulls out a canister of pepper spray.

"You ever have to use that?" Mari asks.

"More than you think. This one time I was riding with this trucker. We're talking and getting to know each other just fine. Then I look over, and his dick's out. It's just there. Standing straight up like a little one-eyed monster waiting to devour me."

"Gross," Mari says. "So you sprayed him?"

"Not yet. I just asked him to put his penis away and let me out. He ignored my first request but pulled over. Then, he reached over like he was going to unlock the door. Instead, he grabbed the back of my head and tried to shove my face into his crotch."

"Ugh," Mari says.

"That's when I sprayed the fucker."

"Damn," Archie says.

She nods. "Moral of the story: always travel with pepper spray."

Dante asks, "So why do you keep doing it?"

She shrugs. "I'm a wanderer. It's who I am. I've learned to accept that a bit of danger comes with the territory. I just try to make good decisions about who I ride with and be prepared just in case I'm wrong."

The conversation sinks into silence. Mari turns the radio up and scans the stations, but it's still all country. The world hums under the tires.

"So we told you what's in Seattle," Archie says. "What's in Chicago? A boyfriend?"

"No boyfriend," Sunshine laughs. "I like girls."

Dante sits up, watching to see how his friends will react.

"That's cool," Mari says.

"Oh," Archie says, disappointed.

Sam doesn't say anything.

"Don't actually know anyone in Chicago," Sunshine says.

"So why go there?" Mari asks.

Sunshine shrugs. "I am a Disciple of the Road, I guess."

"Where are you from?" asks Mari.

Sunshine shrugs again. "Everywhere. Nowhere."

Sam rolls his eyes.

"Why don't you come to Seattle with us?" Archie asks.

Mari turns to him in disbelief.

"Sweet of you to offer," Sunshine says, "but one thing about life on the road is that there's no use over-planning, no use fighting for control. You have to learn to go where the road takes you.

To let go of what you think matters when you must. To accept the fact that you can't see over the next hill. This hill? It's telling me Chicago."

"Do you have a job?" Sam asks.

"Being one with the Universe."

"Does that pay well?" Archie asks with a smile.

"Better than most people realize."

Sam scoffs. "So how do you buy anything? How do you get anywhere?"

"Blowjobs mostly," Sunshine says.

Everyone raises an eyebrow. Archie clears his throat and drops his voice an octave to ask, "Really?"

Mari slaps his shoulder, causing the car to swerve a bit.

"No," Sunshine says, laughing. "Not really. I'm gay, remember?"

Archie deflates.

Sunshine peeks around Sam and looks at Dante. "You are, too, yeah?"

Everyone looks at Dante. His face hot, he drops his eyes and shakes his head. "Um. No."

"Huh," Sunshine says. "My gaydar's usually pretty reliable."

Mari notices Dante shift in his seat. "Anyone need to pee?" she asks, changing the subject. "I think there's a rest stop coming up."

After a few more miles, they spot the signs. When they reach the exit, they pull into the rest area, which is crowded with Saturday travelers. After nearly crashing into several cars and almost hitting some poor, unsuspecting family, Archie successfully parks. It is a crooked, minor miracle. Everyone piles out and sucks in the fresh air.

They stretch their limbs, and Archie hands the keys back to Mari.

"Ten minutes," Sam says and then walks away, a cigarette already between his lips.

Archie, Dante, Mari, and Sunshine stroll toward the main building together until the path splits toward the men's and women's restrooms.

"Sorry about Sam," Mari says as she walks inside with Sunshine.

"Nothing to be sorry for. He's just hurting," Sunshine says, heading into a stall.

Mari picks the one next to her, arranges toilet paper around the seat, and then sits.

"But," Sunshine calls from her stall, "he does need to learn that women are not items to be 'won.' That's probably a large part of the reason she dumped him. But he'll probably learn that soon enough."

Mari considers whether she wants to participate in a conversation while urinating. "Yeah," she finally says. Thankfully, Sunshine doesn't add anything further.

They both flush, emerge from their stalls at the same time, and then walk over to the sinks.

"So what's going on with you and Archie?" Sunshine asks.

Mari keeps her eyes focused on the water. "What about us?"

"I might have been wrong about Dante, but I'm not wrong about you guys. It's pretty obvious. What I don't get is why you're both pretending like there's nothing there."

"I don't know," Mari admits, meeting Sunshine's eyes in the mirror. "It's kind of weird. We hung out the other night. It was nice, but things got weird. And we haven't talked about it yet or anything."

"Why not?"

"I think we both just have too much going on in our lives right now. Bad timing, you know?"

"But wouldn't it be nice to have someone to go through that stuff with?" Sunshine asks.

Mari considers this.

"You have a convenient excuse," Sunshine says, taking a paper towel from the wall dispenser. She dries her hands, balls the paper, and tosses it into the garbage. "But the heart doesn't give a fuck about timing."

"You don't understand."

"Whatever." Sunshine pulls a small baggie out of her purse and then a square of thin paper. Mari realizes that she's about to roll a joint. "Want to smoke up?" Sunshine asks, noticing Mari staring.

"Um, no, thanks. I'll see you back at the car."

One Hill at a Time

The downtown Chicago skyline looms on the other side of the water. The sun hangs high overhead. Seagulls swoop in wide circles, chattering and squawking.

Archie, Sam, Dante, and Mari sit on the tiered cement steps that stretch the length of the pier in front of the planetarium. They drink in the view, enjoying the feel of the wind and the scent of the fresh lake air. Children hop on and off the steps around them, balloons tied to their wrists.

Dante looks down at the book in his hands. The edges of the pages are dyed red. He examines the worn, black cover. It features a small, square abstract painting with the title of the book below it in misaligned words. *The Road* by Jack Kerouac. *A little heavy-handed*, Dante thinks.

He pulls out a scrap of paper tucked between the pages like a bookmark. It contains the contact information for Sunshine's friends in Minnesota.

Sam snatches the novel from Dante's hands and flips through it. "I can't believe this is all she gave us. We drive her a couple hundred miles, and she can't even pay for a tank of gas?"

Archie steals the book from Sam and then hands it back to Dante.

"I liked her," Dante says, smoothing his hand over the book's cover. "She was honest."

"Too bad she was a lesbian," Archie says.

Mari asks, "So what?"

Archie holds up his hands in mock surrender. "Just kidding. Geez. Don't hit me." He starts giggling.

"What?" Mari asks.

"Sorry, I was just remembering that time Sam got punched. Remember, Sam? The first year we played D&D, when we used to use Ms. Prescott's classroom after school."

"Yeah," Sam says, looking away. "I remember."

How could he forget the first time in his life he was really hit hard? After the punch he had slumped in the empty school hallway, closed his eyes, and leaned back against the lockers. His hair was a mess. His left cheek was bright with broken blood vessels and continuing to swell. Blood trickled from his nose, staining his white shirt with droplets so dark they looked brown—nothing like the bright red in the movies.

His backpack was on the ground a few feet away, ripped open, its contents scattered across the floor like an archipelago. Pain radiated from the center of his face. His vision was blurry. He felt like he was going to throw up.

Bearing a handful of paper towels, Archie had been the first on the scene. And then Dante, and then Mari. Was Sarah there? He can't recall. But he does remember the blood. It seemed like it would never stop. He was worried he'd run out. Not long after he had pressed a fresh wad of paper towels to his nose, it would be soaked completely through.

And then Mari had pulled out a tampon. It was the first time any of the boys had ever seen one up close. At first, in its white plastic, he thought it might be a small popsicle or something. But then she ripped open the packaging and pushed the plunger on the plastic applicator, exposing the stubby, condensed wad of cotton with a string dangling from the end. The boys cringed, recognizing it from sex ed. Then Mari had cut it in half with a pair of scissors that Archie grabbed from a classroom, and she shoved a segment into each of Sam's nostrils.

Archie had taken a picture with his phone.

Everyone must remember this at the same time, because sitting on the steps overlooking Lake Michigan, they all start laughing. Even Sam.

"I wonder if I still have that picture," Archie says, shaking with laugher.

"Remind me," Mari says, "why'd that kid punch you?"

"I don't even remember," Sam says.

"I do," Archie says. "The kid called me a 'geeky fag.' So Sam pushed him."

Mari shakes her head. "Boys."

"Oh, please," Archie says. "You just don't understand what it's like to grow up male in this world."

Mari raises her eyebrows. "Enlighten me."

"It's just like in Warcraft," Archie says. "Nobody's going to mess with the leveled-up, badass-looking avatar. They're too afraid. So they skirt around him, let him do as he pleases. Meanwhile, the noobs and mid-levels have to be vigilant, or they'll be torn apart. It's a simple matter of survival of the fittest."

"That's just a video game, Arch."

"That's real life, too, Mari. And despite our morality and our intellect, it'll always be that way for guys. We're evolutionarily hardwired to respect strength and despise weakness. I'm not saying I agree with it. That's just the way it is."

Mari shakes her head. "It's only that way because you guys believe it has to be that way."

"Don't hate the player," Archie says. "Hate the game."

"He's right," Sam says.

Dante nods.

"Of course I'm right," Archie says. "So what are our options? One: find a body switching device and trade with Dante. Two: lift weights and pray for a growth spurt. Three: bide our time, hone our intelligence, and then crush our male competitors with our eventual economic success. Personally, I think I'm making progress on the latter two fronts."

"And they say girls are vain." Mari says. "Wait—I don't remember—was Sarah there?"

"No," Sam answers, finally remembering. "She was at a student council meeting or something. Anyways, let's get going. We've wasted enough time."

"But there's so much to do here," Archie says, arms outstretched toward the city. "Deep dish pizza. That giant silver bean. Da Bears. Let's see the sights, stay the night, and be on our way in the morning."

"Do we have enough money for all of that?" Mari asks.

Archie drops his arms. "No."

Sam stands. "We can stop to eat here on the way back."

Dante nods and rises. Archie sighs. Mari walks over, takes one of his hands, and leads him back to the car.

"One hill at a time, Arch," she says. "One hill at a time."

Surprised by the Spinning World

SATURDAY, 9:10 P.M.

"Shit. Anybody have signal?" Sam says.

He waves his phone around as if it will make a difference.

It does not.

Everyone checks their phones and finds the same problem.

"So where am I supposed to go?" Dante asks, turning off the radio and peering into the night.

"If I remember the map correctly," Archie says, "we've only got a couple more turns. For now, just keep on keepin' on."

Dante rubs his eyes to better concentrate on the portion of the narrow dirt road illuminated by the headlights. Dense trees press in on either side, and beyond that, darkness and silence.

Mari yawns. "We haven't seen another car in like an hour. I think we've pushed our luck too far. We're definitely getting murdered this time."

"Don't blame me. I wanted to keep driving," Sam says, leaning back.

"Need I remind you we're all sleep deprived? You're welcome to take the wheel," Mari says.

Sam doesn't respond.

"Here," Archie says, pointing to an unmarked intersection up ahead. "Go right."

Dante brings the car to a stop and looks where a street sign should be. "Are you sure?"

Archie closes his eyes and rubs his temples with his forefingers as if divining truth. "Yes."

Dante turns to Mari and Sam in the back seat. Sam continues looking out the window. Mari nods. Dante sighs, rubs the tiredness out of his eyes once more, and turns right.

The road narrows even further, as though it is fighting a losing a battle against the surrounding vegetation. Some creature darts across their path.

"Yup," Mari says, tilting her head to find the moon through the tangle of branches overhead. "Murdered."

A few minutes later, they begin to traverse a series of small hills. Rising and dipping and curving around blind corners, they drive in silence. The road then settles into a gradual ascent that peaks after a mile or so. They follow it downhill until it opens up.

"We're on a bridge," Mari says.

The trees on either side have disappeared. In their place is a dark body of water, its vastness measurable by points of light that could be houses or campfires that ring its shores. Above them, the sky is clear and crowded with stars and a moon fat with light.

Archie sits up and readjusts his glasses. "Yeah, I remember this on the map. Lake Somethingrather. Hang a left once we cross the bridge and then that should take us to the guy's house."

Dante follows Archie's directions and soon enough they find themselves on the correct route. They scan the mailboxes that line the road, and it's not long before they locate the house number of their destination. Dante turns down the drive, steers them along its long and winding track, and then parks next to a couple of other cars that sit in front of a large house that looks like an upscale log cabin.

"You're welcome," Archie says.

They all hop out of the car and stretch. The droning buzz of insects reverberates through the air.

They make their way to the front door, and Mari rings the bell. "Here's to getting murdered." She winks at Archie.

They wait for several moments, but nobody answers. Mari presses the button again. They hear a chime within, but nobody comes to the door.

"Let's just go to a hotel," Sam says.

"We don't have enough money," Archie says.

"Then we can sleep in the car at a rest stop," Sam says.

Just as Mari's about to knock, they hear a burst of distant laughter.

"They must be outside," she says and then starts walking around the house. The others follow her, too tired to argue.

Turning the corner, they find four men reclining in lawn chairs around a bonfire, drinking from red plastic cups. Their smiling faces are lit by the orange glow of the fire. One of them says something and they all break out in laughter. Beyond a small cluster of trees, the lake's presence downhill can be felt more than seen.

Mari and the others stop several feet away. She clears his throat. "Ahem. Excuse me, gentlemen . . ."

The laughter and conversation die down. The four men turn toward their visitors.

"Can we help you?" one of them says, his voice deep and even. He has a beard and is smoking a pipe.

Archie looks at his friends. "We're . . . umm . . ."

"We're Sunshine's friends," Mari says.

"Who?" the bearded pipe smoker asks. He looks at his friends and then back to Mari.

"Sunshine—we spoke to one of you on the phone—Zaius?"

One of the other men rises from his seat and approaches. He seems to be in his thirties, and he's built like a professional baseball player—tall and vaguely athletic.

"We don't know no Sunshine or Zaius," he says. He spits in the direction of the trees and then takes a long drink from his cup. "I think you all got the wrong house."

"Sorry to disturb you . . . we'll be on our way," Archie says.

He starts to back up but then bumps into someone. He turns around and comes face to face with the other two guys who, having left their places at the fire, must have circled around and snuck up behind them. One is skinny and short, grinning to reveal gleaming, white teeth. The other is fat and unsmiling.

"Why do you think they're in such a rush, eh?" the skinny guy says.

The fat guy eyeballs them. "Don't know. Maybe they don't like our company."

Archie gulps. He looks around at his friends who seem equally confused. They move closer together.

"Look," Dante says, putting his hands up in surrender. "We don't want any trouble. If you just—"

"Just what, big guy?" asks the baseball player. He gets nose-to-nose with Dante, the two standing at nearly the same height. He raises a fist and Dante flinches. The man grins, lowers his arm, and steps back. "This here is private property. And you're trespassing."

The bearded guy takes a puff from his pipe, still seated at the fire. "They have to pay the price."

"Fuck you," Sam says. He moves to walk away, but the fat guy blocks his path. Sam stares him down but thinks better of it and rejoins his friends.

"As we were saying," says the skinny guy, still smirking. "The price."

"What is it?" Archie asks. "We don't have much money."

The skinny guy looks over at the bearded guy who nods.

"Her," the skinny guy says, tilting his chin toward Mari.

Mari straightens up. She folds her arms over her chest. She wishes she had some pepper spray. "As my friend said a moment ago: Fuck you."

The bearded guy taps his pipe against the plastic arm of his lawn chair, knocking out the spent tobacco. He gets up, walks over, and stands directly in front of Mari. He leans forward until his face is almost touching her hair. He inhales deeply.

Dante and Archie move to rush at him, but the baseball player and the fat guy shove them backward, toward the fire. The skinny guy keeps his eyes locked on Sam, who keeps glancing at the car.

The fire crackles. A bird calls from the darkness.

The bearded man pulls his face away and leers at Mari. He smells of smoke and beer.

Mari meets his eyes. She wishes she had the car keys so she could arrange them between her fingers like claws and rake the man across his grinning face.

"Don't even think about touching her," Archie says.

"Too late," says the skinny guy.

"Or what?" asks the fat guy.

Archie meets each of their eyes in turn. "Or I'll kill you."

The men look at each other and then break out in uncontrollable laughter. At first it seems as if they're laughing at Archie. But when they continue, doubling over with tears in their eyes, slapping each other on the back, it becomes clear there's some other joke. Archie, Mari, Dante, and Sam exchange confused looks.

The bearded guy walks over to Archie and puts his hand on his shoulder. He takes a deep breath to regain his composure. "We're just fucking with you," he says. He and his friends are all smiling in a way that's no longer menacing. "I'm Zaius. Short for Isaias."

He holds out his hand. Archie looks at it. "For real?"

"For real," he answers.

Archie, Mari, Dante, and Sam look at each other and let out a collective sigh of relief. The tension dissolves. Archie shakes Zaius's hand.

"I'm Clark," says the skinny guy.

"Adam," says the fat one, nodding.

"Lamont," says the guy built like a baseball player.

Mari, Archie, Dante, and Sam introduce themselves, and then they follow Zaius back to the fire. He walks over to a keg that rests in a tub of ice and begins filling cups and passing them around. "Welcome to our humble abode."

Sam immediately begins downing his drink, as Archie, Dante, and Mari examine the foamy, golden beverage in their cups.

"Thanks," Mari says. "I don't mean to be rude . . . but we've been driving all day and it's kind of late. Maybe you can just show us where we can sleep?"

"You can sleep when you're dead," Zaius says. "You're travelers. So travel." He raises his cup and his friends do the same.

"We're not twenty-one," Archie says.

Zaius shrugs and takes a drink. "We live in a country where as soon as you turn eighteen the government will ship you overseas to murder strangers. Who cares about some bullshit drinking age?" He looks over at Sam, who's already tilting his head back to catch the last drops from his cup. "Just have some self-control."

"He's got a point," Mari says. She takes a sip and then makes a face. But then takes another.

Dante and Archie follow suit.

"Sorry, but we only have so many chairs," Zaius says moving back to his own. "But we can make room for you."

Clark sits on Adam's lap, while Lamont drops to the ground in front of Zaius and leans back against his legs. They hold hands and then Zaius kisses Lamont on the top of the head.

Noticing the looks of surprise on Dante's and Archie's faces, Zaius asks, "Didn't Sunshine tell you?" When nobody answers, he says, "We're married."

Sam pours himself another cup of beer and then plops down into one of the empty chairs. "All four of you?" he asks, more interested in the cigarette he's now trying to light. "Like one big, gay family?"

"No," Adam says, laughing. "Clark and I are married to each other, and Lamont is with Zaius."

Archie gestures for Mari to take the other seat and then sits cross-legged on the ground next to her. Dante stays on his feet, staring into the flames, watching them flicker and curl in on themselves. "It's legal here?" he asks after a moment.

"Yup," says Zaius. "Since 2013. We were the sixth and seventh couples in line for certificates in St. Paul as soon as it was announced."

"The old regime of bigotry is falling like dominoes," says Clark. "It's a whole new world."

"That's how we know Sunshine," Lamont adds. "Back in college, we all volunteered for an organization that fought for marriage equality."

Mari smiles at them. "It must be amazing to see your work pay off like this."

"You have no idea," Zaius says. "Just imagine an entire generation never having to hear that they can't marry the person they love. Never having to feel like they're less than human." He puts down his drink, packs fresh tobacco into his pipe, and then relights it. After it catches, he tosses the match into the bonfire and starts rubbing Lamont's broad shoulders. "Makes all those hours we spent standing on street corners annoying people for signatures worth it."

Dante takes a drink and looks at Archie, who looks away.

"Don't you get shit from people?" Archie asks.

Zaius smiles. "Don't you?"

Archie doesn't respond.

"So what are you guys? Like a band on tour or something?" Clark asks.

"No," Mari answers. "Just friends."

"That's cool. How did you all meet?" Lamont asks.

"We go to the same school," she says.

"At least, we did," Archie adds.

"But I mean, like, how did you start hanging out? There's probably a lot of fucking kids in your school, right?"

"Dungeons & Dragons," Mari explains. "We started playing together in sixth grade."

Clarks says, "That's that game with the dice and the . . . uh . . . the dragons . . . and the . . ."

"Dungeons," Mari finishes. "Yes."

"You still play?" Lamont asks.

They nod.

He laughs. "That's one long-ass game."

"You have no idea," Mari says.

"So you're a bunch of nerds on a real life adventure," Zaius says. He notices that Sam seems offended, so he smiles. "In this world, you've got to know who you are, and you've got to own it."

Dante meets his eyes. "Otherwise?"

"Otherwise, what's the point?"

Dante turns back to the fire and takes a drink, starting to feel pleasantly light and dizzy.

"Hey, what time is it?" Clark asks, smirking.

Several of them check their phones, but there's still no signal, so they shake their heads.

"Time to swim," Clark says. He puts down his cup, pulls off his shirt, and sprints into the darkness. They hear his feet stomping across the wood of the dock, and then a moment later, the splash of water.

Without hesitation, Adam rips off his shirt, revealing a wondrous belly, and follows after his husband. Again, there's the hollow sound of steps across wooden planks punctuated by a splash, this time much louder.

"You coming?" Zaius asks as he and Lamont rise to join their friends. "Summer's almost over, but water's still great. Plus, the bugs aren't nearly as bad anymore."

"That's because of the bats," Lamont adds, smiling.

The couple walks toward the lake. Mari, Dante, Archie, and Sam hesitate.

"Fuck that," Sam says, moving over to the keg to fill his cup a third time. "I'm staying here where there's heat and beer."

"I'll stay, too," Dante says, yawning.

Mari turns to Archie, "What do you say, Arch?"

Archie downs what's left in his cup, nods at her, and then stands. "Whoa," he says, surprised by the spinning world.

He stumbles and Mari catches him. "Lightweight," she says.

She laces her fingers through his, and they walk down to the lake together.

Dante takes one of the empty seats and then sits with Sam in silence. Enjoying the sensation of being buzzed for the first time in his life, he watches the flames form and reform. Sam alternates between smoking and drinking. The soft sounds of splashing and laughter float through the evening air.

"I'm sick of them already," Sam says.

"Who?" Dante asks. "Zaius and his friends?"

Sam shakes his head. "Archie and Mari."

"I like it," Dante says. "They're good for each other."

"Nobody's good for anybody."

Dante resolves to leave it at that, but can't help himself from taking the bait. "What's wrong with them?"

"It's not them in particular. It's just that all girls are terrible."

Dante looks at Sam. "All?"

"Yes," Sam answers into his cup. "All."

"I don't—"

"Mari will make him fall in love with her, and then she'll rip his still-beating heart from his chest and devour it right in front of the poor bastard."

"Why do I get the feeling you're talking about you and Sarah?"

"It's just the way things are, man. The way of the world," Sam says, his words starting to slur. "Maybe I should just turn gay, ya know? Like these dudes. Clark and Adam and Lamont or whatever and that guy with the beard with the Z name. Dr. Zaius. They seem to have it all figured out. Fuck women. They're all evil."

"But—"

"All of 'em. Every last one. If it has a vagina, it's evil. To be honest, I think those things must be like vortexes to hell. Yeah, hellmouths. That's what we should start calling them. Little hellmouths. Lurking between their legs. And, like, once a dick enters them it, like, releases demons and spirits and leprechauns and all kinds of other evil shit. Pandora's Pussy, ya know?"

Sam finishes his beer and stumbles back to the keg.

Dante rises to help him back to his seat. "Maybe you've had enough for tonight, Sam."

Sam dances away from Dante's hands. "No, no, I'm good. I'm great. Feeling better than ever before." He tilts his head back and howls to the moon. "*Ah-wooooooooooooo!*"

"You guys alright up there?" Zaius calls from the lake.

"Fucking great!" Sam shouts back, his words echoing. "Fuck women! Fuck their hellmouths!" He giggles.

Dante again tries to guide Sam back to his seat, but Sam dodges his grasp. In doing so, he trips over himself and stumbles onto his ass. The cigarette falls from his mouth, so he takes out a new one and lights it. Laughing, he finally accepts Dante's help back into his chair.

"You're a good friend, Dante," Sam says, slouching so low that he's nearly sliding off his seat.

"Thanks, Sam."

"We never really say shit like that, right? Because we're guys or whatever. But fuck that, ya know? It's true. Let's stop with the fake shit. Let's only speak the truth for the rest of our lives. You're, like, just so nice when everyone else is so fucking mean and selfish. I love it. I love you, man."

"Um, thanks."

"No, no, I mean it. Like, nobody else is staying up here with me to make sure I'm not drinking myself to death, ya know?"

Dante looks up at the sky. "They've got their own stuff going on, too, Sam."

Sam points his cigarette at Dante. "See? There you go again, being fucking nicer than people deserve. Putting everyone before Dante. But know what I appreciate most about you, big guy?"

"What?"

"You've got a penis. Not one of those evil hellmouths. Seriously, man. I mean it. I'm going gay. Fuck girls. Fuck Sarah." He raises his cup for a toast. "To penis!"

"You should go to bed."

"To penis!" Sam says, more loudly this time, cup still raised.

"Sam—"

"Say it, motherfucker—to penis!"

Dante sighs, and raises his cup. "To penis."

"Louder."

"No."

171

"*To penis!*" Sam shouts.

"Here, here!" someone calls from the lake.

"I'm not yelling it like that," says Dante.

"I'm gonna keep screaming it till you do. *To penis! To penis! Tooooo peeeeeenissss!*"

"*To penis!*" Dante finally yells, unable to resist smiling as he does so.

Sam smiles and lifts his cup even higher. "*And balls!*"

"*And balls!*" Dante echoes, laughing.

Sam smiles and knocks his cup against Dante's. Dante uses the opportunity to ease Sam's cup out of his hands before he can bring it back to his lips.

Sam lets it happen and then laughs into a sigh. "But you know what, big guy? I don't know if I could really do it. Be gay, you know." He makes a face. Drops his voice to a whisper, "Can you imagine putting it down there? Like, it doesn't bother me at all that people are gay. I mean, do whatever the fuck you want, ya know? Who are we to tell anyone what to do with their junk? Just don't hurt anyone."

"I guess," Dante says.

"Nobody can tell someone else who to bang or not bang."

Dante grabs a piece of firewood from a nearby pile and places it into the flames, sending a puff of embers drifting into the air. They burn out, and he relaxes a bit as he senses Sam's energy flagging.

"Good talk. I'm gonna go throw up now," Sam says, rising from his chair unsteadily.

"Here, let me—"

"You gotta stop being so fucking nice all the time," Sam says, pointing a wavering finger. "I mean. Don't get me wrong. I appreciate your concern and all. Like I said, I love you for it, big guy. But I'm not too bad. Just had one too many. So sometimes you need to help, and sometimes you just need to let people vomit by themselves in a corner."

"Is this one of those times?"

"It is."

And with that, Sam stumbles away, leaving Dante by the fire. Dante listens to Sam's progress through the trees, resisting the urge to help. He relaxes once he hears the house door creak open and then slam shut.

He sits by himself for a moment longer, considering whether he should head into the house and go to sleep, wait for the others to return, or join them at the lake.

Finishing his beer, he stands and decides to leave the warmth and light. He follows the voices down a narrow dirt path through the darkness and trees to the dock. Lit by the moonlight, he sees six heads bobbing in the calm, dark water.

"All right! It's Heavy D," Archie says. "Jump in, man."

"Yeah, jump in, Dante," Mari encourages.

Clark starts chanting, "*Jump in! Jump in!*" The others pick it up, their voices loud enough to wake everyone around the lake.

Dante shakes his head and sits at the end of the dock next to several small piles of clothing. He removes his shoes and socks, and dips his feet into the water. It is warmer than the air.

"Boo," Archie says.

"Hey," Mari says, "leave him alone. He'll get in when he's ready."

She then jumps on Archie's back and tries to push his head into the lake. The struggle takes them both underwater. They break the surface a moment later, dripping and sputtering and laughing.

"I've got something to tell you guys," Dante says, eyes fixed on moonlight glimmering in the water's surface.

"What's that?" Archie asks.

Dante hesitates. He doesn't know why. If there's anywhere he can say it, it would be here, tonight. Instead, he lifts his feet out of the water. "Um . . . it's Sam."

"He all right?" Zaius asks while treading water next to Lamont. "He seemed to be hitting the bottom of that cup pretty hard. I should probably be a responsible adult and cut him off."

"Oh, he'll be fine. Went inside to get some of it out of his system and then sleep. Just thought you should know."

Zaius nods. "Make sure you keep an eye on that one, alright? He seems fairly bent on self-destruction."

"What's his deal?" Clark asks, arms clinging around Adam's wide neck.

"What do you mean?" Dante asks.

"He's kind of a dick is what I mean."

"Oh, that. Long story."

"No it's not," Archie interjects. "He's just sad. He got dumped. We're on our way to help him win her back. The end." He turns to Mari. "We just should just get him a T-shirt that explains that."

"So do you think it's going to work?" Clark asks. "Not the T-shirt. The girlfriend thing."

Dante and Archie and Mari exchange skeptical glances. Nobody speaks, and their silence is enough of an answer.

Zaius asks, "So why go with him?"

"He's one of us," Archie says.

"Well," Zaius says, "in my opinion, there are only two kinds of travelers: those who are going somewhere, and those who are running from something. Sam is clearly the former. Which kind are you guys?"

"We," says Mari, "are here."

Archie nods, head bobbing just above the water's surface. "We are here. Hundreds of miles from home, under a sky full of stars, going for a midnight swim with four gay dudes—no offense."

"None taken. We are, in fact, gay dudes," Lamont says.

Then Mari says, "The world is so much bigger than it was on Friday."

Lamont nods. "Travelling helps you see that. The world is bigger than you think."

"You know what else is bigger than you think?" Archie asks, grinning.

Everyone groans and Mari swats at him. Archie blocks it and then wraps up her arms in a bear hug to prevent another attack.

"Think it's about time we head in, guys. What do you say?" Zaius asks.

"I'm actually pretty aw—" Lamont starts to say but is interrupted by Zaius's elbow. "Oh, actually . . ." Lamont yawns. "Yup, time to hit the hay."

Zaius shoots a meaningful look at Clark and Adam, and they echo Lamont's sentiment. All four swim to the dock and pull themselves out of the water. Dante averts his eyes, but the moonlight helps him realize that they're all nude.

As they gather their bundles of clothes, dripping onto the dock, Archie and Mari start swimming back in. But Zaius holds up a hand. "You two should stay out here for a little longer. Let yourselves in the house whenever you're ready. The couch in the sunroom is all yours."

Archie looks to Mari and then back to Zaius. "Cool. Um . . . are there, like, extra blankets so I can sleep on the floor?"

"Nope," Zaius says and winks at Mari. "You'll have to share. Come on, Dante. Let us retire to the smoking room."

Dante looks at Mari and Archie, who shrug. He lets Zaius lead him away.

"Just watch out for the bats," Lamont offers over his shoulder.

A few moments later, Mari and Archie find themselves completely alone. An immense hush settles over the lake. They breathe in the silence, feeling as though they've outlasted the insects and animals. The world is vast, and it is theirs. Religions have been founded upon less.

"They seem happy," Archie says, breaking the spell.

"Who? Zaius and the others?" Mari asks.

"Yeah, them."

"Why wouldn't they be?"

Archie lets himself sink a little, until his chin touches the water. He thinks of his own father. "I don't know . . . but, hey, I was right."

"About what?"

"I told you we wouldn't be murdered."

Mari splashes a bit of water at him. "Not yet. But we are swimming in the middle of the night by ourselves—isn't that, like, the opening of every horror movie ever? Let's hold off on celebrating our survival."

"No," Archie says, sending a return splash her way. "As long as we're alive, let's never stop celebrating the simple fact that we are alive."

Mari laughs and then stares at Archie, wondering if he somehow knows about her mom. Deciding his words were coincidence, she drifts away with a lazy backstroke. "So is that your grand epiphany?"

"Is that what?" he asks, closing the distance between them.

"You should be freaking out about missing school. Realistically, we're probably not going to make it back until next week. Aren't you concerned about your GPA? Your chance to reign as valedictorian at your new school?"

"Am I really that guy?"

"You were. But something's different." She lets her legs sink and starts treading water. *"As long as we're alive, let's never stop celebrating the simple fact that we are alive,"* she quotes, mocking Archie's voice.

"Is that supposed to be me?"

"They're your words."

He laughs, caught in so many ways. "Don't make fun of me. Just seemed like the right thing to say at the time."

"It was."

They let the quietness rebuild.

Mari drifts toward Archie until she is floating in front of him. She puts her arms around his neck, and their bodies press together as they tread water. Under the surface, Archie touches one hand to her hips. She does not pull away.

They touch foreheads. Their eyeglasses clink together. Mari takes Archie's hand and they paddle back to the small pier. She removes both their glasses and places them on the dock. Pulling Archie closer, she sits on the lowest step of the ladder so that they can hold each other in the water without sinking to the bottom of the lake.

"I'm sorry about the other night," he says. "Whatever I did to ruin it, I'm sorry."

"It's not your fault," Mari says in a whisper. "You just said something that made me remember something bad."

"What?"

Mari hesitates. She looks up at the full moon. Finds the face in it. "My mom has cancer . . ."

Archie drifts closer to her. "Mari . . . I'm so sorry . . . is it bad?"

"Is cancer ever good?" Mari asks.

"That was stupid . . . I'm sorry . . ." Archie says.

"Stop apologizing. It's okay. I mean, it will be okay. Hopefully."

"Do you want to talk about it?"

"Not right now. It's enough just to know that you know."

"Why didn't you tell us?" he asks.

She shrugs. "We never really talk about that kind of stuff."

"Yeah," Archie says. "We'll start, okay?"

"Okay."

"Archie?"

"Yes, Mari?"

"Am I a terrible person?" she asks in a whisper again.

"Why would you ask that?" he asks, also whispering.

"Because I'm here. Doing this."

"You're helping a friend," he says.

"Maybe. Or maybe I'm just avoiding her. Avoiding what she wants me to do . . . when she might be dying."

"What does she want you to do?" Archie asks.

She lowers her eyes. Sidles closer. "It's not important right now."

Archie chooses his next words carefully. "You're not a terrible person, Mari. You're the most amazing person I know. And I don't think your mom would want you to stop living life. In fact, just the opposite."

She nods. "You're probably right."

Archie leans in to kiss her, but she pulls away.

"If we do this, it will change everything," she says.

"I hope so," he says.

She looks at him. He looks at her. Without their glasses, they are fuzzy to each other. That somehow makes this easier.

Mari leans forward. She presses her lips to his.

And, somewhere, there really are bats.

But not here, not now.

There is nothing except this.

Yes and No

SUNDAY, 5:45 A.M.

An overcast sky in the morning replaces the clarity of last night. A cool breeze rustles the leaves, carrying a suggestion of rain.

As they load the car, Mari and Archie exchange flirtatious glances, Dante is lost deep in thought, and Sam groans at the wrath of a hangover.

"I'll tell the others you said goodbye," says Zaius. "They would've liked to see you off, but you know how it is." He gestures toward Sam. "He does, at least."

Sam mutters his appreciation as he climbs into the front seat and rolls down the window.

Mari slams the trunk and hugs Zaius, kissing him on the cheek. "Thank you for everything."

"Anytime."

She moves back to Archie and slides her arm around his waist.

"Seriously, thanks," Archie says, smiling.

Dante nods and shakes Zaius's hand.

"Seriously," Zaius says, "if you need a place to stop on your way back, you're welcome here. The road can be a lonely place."

Mari laughs. "But we're not traveling alone."

Zaius shrugs. "Yes and no."

The Edge of the World

SUNDAY, 9:57 A.M.

As they cross the state line, the sky darkens into a greenish hue. Towering storm clouds push the late morning light into a sliver on the horizon. The rain picks up, and Dante sets the wipers swinging back and forth at their highest setting in a futile attempt to clear the droplets that batter the windshield.

He clicks on the headlights and tightens his grip on the steering wheel. He struggles to hold the road as gusts of winds push the car toward the shoulder. His visibility reduced, he slows the car to a crawl. He squints to find the dashed lines.

There are a few other vehicles on the road, and though they've slowed down, they're still moving fast enough to overtake Dante.

None of his friends are aware of his struggle. Sam is fast asleep in the front seat. Mari and Archie sleep in the back, holding hands while her head rests in his lap.

Just as Dante's about to wake them, the rain dampens to a steady drizzle, restoring his view. Flat fields of brown and pale green slide by on either side. The menacing clouds still hang overhead, flickering from within.

Suddenly, there's a flash of red, immediately followed by a deafening crack of thunder that seems to shake the world.

Mari's and Archie's eyes pop open. Sam remains asleep.

Mari removes herself from Archie's arms and sits up. "What the hell was that?" she asks, her voice groggy. "We hit something?"

Dante tilts his chin in the direction of the road ahead. "Storm. Looks pretty bad."

"Where are we?" Archie asks, rubbing the sleep from his eyes and stretching as best as he can in the confined space.

"Crossed into North Dakota about half an hour ago."

Archie puts on his glasses and then leans forward for a better look. "I have a bad feeling about this."

Another thunderclap booms overhead. The rain's intensity redoubles. The sky grows even darker, giving the impression that it's midnight instead of midday.

"I might need to pull over," Dante says.

"Fuck that," Sam mutters, eyes still closed. He hugs his pillow and sinks back to sleep.

"I hate to say this," Archie says, "but I think this might be a tornado."

Dante looks at him in the rearview mirror. "Tell me you're joking."

"I used to be really into meteorology," Archie says. "Weather patterns are fascinating. Probably some of the most complex math there is. So many variables and—"

"Get to the point, Arch," Mari interrupts.

Archie points out the window. "Look at those clouds. Dark. Low hanging, but towering. They're cumulonimbus. They make tornadoes."

"Maybe it's just a really bad thunderstorm," says Mari. Dante shakes his head in disbelief. He steps on the gas.

Archie puts his hand on his shoulder. "Slow down. If we do see a tornado, the worst thing you can do is to keep driving."

"Then what should I do?" he asks, gazing at the threatening clouds.

Archie leans forward and clicks on the radio. Immediately, a woman's urgent voice fills the speakers.

"—Richland, Ransom, Barnes, Cass, Steele, Traill counties until one P.M. Multiple touchdowns have been sighted. If possible, seek shelter immediately. If you are outside, lie flat in the nearest depression, ditch, ravine, or culvert."

There's a series of screeching beeps, and then the message restarts. "The National Weather Service has issued a tornado warning for Richland, Ransom, Barnes . . ."

As the voice loop continues, their eyes all shift to the shallow ditch that runs alongside the road. It does not seem to promise much in the way of protection.

Sam finally opens his eyes. "A *warning* isn't that bad, right? *Watch* is the bad one."

"No, a *warning* is the bad one," says Mari.

Sam shakes his head. "Think about it. Like you *watch* something that's happening. So if there were an actual tornado, it would be a *tornado watch*."

"No, you *watch* for a tornado," Mari says. "Once you see it, you *warn* people."

"Mari's right," Archie says.

"Maybe they're not around here, though," says Sam. "That was a lot of county names they read."

In the distance, they hear an emergency siren whir to life. The pitch of its prolonged whine rises and falls, rises and falls. Though faint, it's a testament to its volume that they're able to hear it through the storm and from within the car.

A few moments later, the sound of the rain transitions from a steady thrum to a sharp staccato. The droplets become little white spheres that bounce off the hood and pavement like golf balls.

"Hail," Archie says. "Big-ass hail. Definitely not a good sign."

"So should I pull over?" Dante asks.

"Keep driving," Sam says, watching the hail fall. "There's not even a funnel-shaped cloud." He closes his eyes again, apparently bored.

Archie points to the north. "You mean like that?"

Dante takes his eyes from the road to see a shadowy smear upon the lighter clouds in the yellow distance beyond a farm-house. At first, it seems motionless. But after a few glances, Dante notices what looks like a dusty cloud. He quickly realizes that it's gathering into a slow spiral. Each time he glances over, the cloud looks more like a funnel.

Mari takes Archie's hand. "Maybe it's moving away from us."

But then the farmhouse disappears within the dark, spinning cloud.

Dante pulls the car onto the shoulder and slams on the brakes. "Everyone out!"

It takes some effort to push open the doors against the wind, but Dante, Mari, and Archie eventually succeed and push into the storm. The world is roaring and shifting. They shield their heads with their arms, sprint to the shallow ravine, and throw themselves into it.

They fail to notice that Sam is still in the car.

The sky flickers with lightning. The thunder grows to an unceasing rumble. Heavy gusts of wind whip dirt and dust through the air. Hail pelts the earth.

Dante lifts his head for a moment and sees what looks like a dark wall of clouds approaching. It is as if he is looking at the edge of the world. He glances at the others to make sure they're still safe. But he only sees Mari and Archie, huddled against each other.

He looks back to the car. Just as he feared, he spots Sam's head pressed against the glass of the window, somehow still asleep.

He glances back at the tornado. The distance between them is closing rapidly. It seems only a minute or two away.

Dante takes a deep breath, hops to his feet, and then rushes to the car using all his strength to push against the wind that seems to come from every direction. He yanks open the door. Startled,

Sam stares at Dante. He opens his mouth to say something, but Dante doesn't wait to hear what—he grabs Sam by the arm and pulls him out of the vehicle.

Dante drags Sam through the wind until they reach the ditch, and then he shoves him down to the ground next to Mari and Archie. Dante lowers himself on top of his friends, stretching out his arms to shield them as much as possible even though it means he can't cover his own head.

Their clothes billow. Dust and dirt whip against Dante's skin. Mari's hair flies in his face.

Frightened and only half-believing in the reality of their situation, he braces for the worst.

The hail seems to cease, but their world becomes the wind. It does not seem possible, but the wind grows even louder, it blows even stronger. It roars and whips the tall grass into a frenzy. It drowns out the universe.

Dante hears something whistle by overhead. Several more objects whizz through the air.

Archie starts to look up, but Dante pushes his head down. A fraction of a second later, another object zooms past, grazing the air just inches above them.

"*I'm so alone*," Sam says.

"*I want my mom*," Mari says.

"*I'm scared*," Archie says.

"*I'm gay*," Dante says.

Suddenly, there's the sound of bursting glass. A moment later, something scrapes across the back of Dante's arms like a hundred razor blades. He grits his teeth. Leaves his head unprotected to cover his friends. They need him now more than ever.

But as suddenly as it started, the wind begins to die down. The rain passes. Silence settles all around them.

Finally, Dante looks up. "It's gone."

The dark funnel has disappeared. The wall of storm clouds has moved on, and in its place are insubstantial, white clouds and a shock of blue sky. Sunlight peeks through. The contrast is surreal.

Dante pushes himself up, uncovering his friends, and falls back onto his butt. Blood trickles down his arms. He feels no pain but knows it's gathering.

Archie and Mari roll onto their backs. They kiss and then look up to watch the sky transform, at once apocalyptic and heavenly.

Sam climbs to his feet. "That was fucking scary," he says. He brushes off the dirt and grass clinging to his clothes. "Well. Let's go."

Dante closes his eyes and says a silent prayer of thanks.

An Arrow Unloosed

SUNDAY, 10:49 A.M.

After he finishes duct taping a semi-transparent plastic garbage bag where the side window used to be, Sam closes the car door and steps back to examine his work.

"See? We don't need to stop. It's fine."

Mari, Dante, and Archie eye the window's sad stand-in.

"Maybe this is a sign that we should go home," Mari says.

"We've already come this far," Sam says. "We can replace it in Seattle. I'll put it on my dad's credit card."

She sighs. "Fine."

"That's what I'm talking about," he says. "And because you're being such a good sport, tell you what: I'll even drive the next leg."

"How generous," she says, and then turns toward Dante. "How's your arm?"

Dante twists his shoulder to reveal a number of red scrapes running the length of his forearm. Rivulets of bright red blood drip down his skin.

Mari moves closer and examines his cuts. "It doesn't look like any pieces are still in there. But let's go clean it. Then we can change into some dry clothes. Get some lunch. My treat."

Dante nods. He heads down the walkway toward the travel center along with Mari and Archie, who are holding hands.

Sam hops onto the trunk of the car and slips a cigarette between his lips. He lights it as he surveys the parking lot, the damp pavement glistening under a bright sun. It is as if there had never been a storm, as if the world had not just nearly taken their lives.

What if it had?

The parking lot is filled with people milling about their cars, talking to strangers about the storm, about what they heard, what they saw, what they know. Even without being part of their conversations, Sam senses the nervous energy, the lingering fear mixed with excitement and coated with disbelief. He feels it, too.

He takes a long drag from his cigarette and then checks his phone. Still no e-mails or texts or calls from Sarah. After the message he left for her last night, he's been expecting something. For better, or for worse.

Sam exhales a puff of smoke and dials her number. It rings a couple of times and then goes to voicemail. He ends the call and then slips the phone back into his pocket.

"Mind if I bum one?" an old man in a trucker hat says as he walks up to Sam. One of the man's shirtsleeves is folded and pinned to the shoulder. He only has one arm.

Without saying anything, Sam hands a cigarette to the man.

"A little help?" the man says, tilting his head toward his missing limb.

"Sorry," Sam says and lights it for him. The old man nods his appreciation as he stands opposite Sam, staring into the distance.

"Hell of a storm," the man says.

Sam nods.

"Largest twister I seen in a long while. Were y'all near it?"

"Kind of," says Sam.

"From what I hear, two young people died up the road. People saying they was just married. Matter of fact, on their way to the airport for their honeymoon." He shakes his head. "A goddamn shame."

"At least they died together," Sam says.

The man lifts his hat and runs a hand through what little hair remains on the top of his head. "Take it from an old man. Don't matter if you got somebody next to you. Every damn person who ever lived died by himself."

"So then what's the point?"

"The point is how you live, not how you die. And you ask me, the way to live is to surround yourself with those you love." The man takes a long drag, letting his old man wisdom sink in. Noticing the car's license plate between Sam's feet, he asks, "A long way from home, eh?"

Sam shrugs.

"Where y'all headed?"

Sam doesn't feel up to explaining where he's going and why he's going there. Maybe a T-shirt would be best. Instead, he just says, "West."

The man nods. "So how you like North Dakota?"

"Besides the fact it just tried to kill me?"

The man laughs. "You can't take it personal, son. It's just weather. It has to get like that sometimes so it can get like this." The man gestures toward the clear skies just as a few birds flit by overhead.

Sam surveys the flat fields. "It felt personal."

"You from the city, eh?

"Kind of."

"Well, just give it a chance," the old man says. "It's actually kind of nice. Quiet enough to think. Space enough to breathe." The man exhales a puff of smoke. "Yup. Born and raised in these fields. I'll probably be buried in them soon enough." He drops his cigarette and snuffs it out with the toe of his boot. "Anyways, a young person like you probably doesn't want to listen to the ramblings of an old, one-armed man like me. You probably got a pretty girlfriend to get back to. But thanks for the smoke and the conversation. You have yourself a good trip, wherever you end up."

"Likewise," Sam says.

The old man nods once more and then walks away.

There's something about the man that reminds him of one of Sarah's uncles. Sam had accompanied Sarah to his wedding last summer. But about halfway through the reception, she disappeared. Left alone, Sam just sat at the table and watched people dance. Her uncle had sat down next to Sam and they talked for a bit. He was actually a pretty interesting guy. Had gone to clown school in Paris before buying a bar in South Philly. Still. He wasn't Sarah.

After her uncle left to mingle with the other guests, Sam had wandered around trying to find Sarah. He finally found her outside. She was out back, on a bench. Sitting on some guy's lap, passing a cigarette back and forth. One of the waiters, she later explained. She knew him back in elementary school, she explained. She also explained that nothing had happened.

Sam believed it at the time. Thinking back on it now, though, he begins to have his doubts.

Sam checks the time on his phone and considers trying Sarah again. But he looks up to find Mari, Archie, and Dante standing next to him. Mari wears a sympathetic expression.

"What's up?" Sam asks.

She holds her phone out to him. "Read it."

It's a long text, split over several messages.

From Sarah.

He reads:

Mari, are you actually on your way here with sam??? i really hope not. i really hope that rambling, incomprehensible message he left for me in the middle of the night was just a drunk dial and nothing more. if you are—TURN AROUND. PLEASE GO BACK HOME. DO NOT COME TO SEATTLE. yes, i love him. yes, i miss him. but it's over. i've told him that. please. i'm not trying to be a bitch. i miss all of you guys and would love everyone to visit. but not like this. not for this. sam and i

are over. that chapter of our lives is done. please help him real-
ize this. if you're really on your way here with him, you're not
helping him. you're enabling him. if you guys want be good
friends, help him move on!!!

Sam lifts his eyes from the screen. Smiles. "She said she loves me. She misses me."

Mari snatches back her cell. "Are you an idiot? Did you read the entire thing?"

Sam hops off the car. "You guys ready?"

"Sam," Dante says. "We need to go home."

"Game over," Archie says.

Sam shakes his head. "This is just the low point in the story. The final test of the hero's resolve."

"Unbelievable," Mari says.

"I'm going to call Sarah and tell her I still love her, too. I'm going to tell her that nothing can stop me."

Sam starts dialing Sarah's number, but Mari slaps him in the side of his head. He drops his phone and it clatters onto the pavement.

"What the fuck?" he asks. He spits out his cigarette, and he picks up the phone. "You broke it." He shows her the screen, now a web of cracked glass.

Mari snatches the phone from his hand and tosses it into the tall grass. "It's for your own good."

Dante runs a hand over the top of his head. "It's over, Sam. We need to go home. I'm sorry." He puts a hand on Sam's shoulder, but Sam shakes it away.

"No. We can't turn around. We can't give up. Not when we're almost there. I haven't won her back yet."

"Let's go, buddy. The psychosis will pass," Archie says.

"Leave him," Dante says. "He just needs to calm down."

Archie, Dante, and Mari walk through the wet grass toward a picnic table.

"Please," Sam begs. "I need to get to Seattle. I need to get to Sarah."

He follows after them and grabs Mari by the arm.

"Just wait, I—"

But before he can finish his sentence, Archie rips his hand off Mari's arm and slams his fist into the side of Sam's head.

Sam stumbles backward and trips to the ground. He stares at Archie. Rubs the spot where his friend struck him.

People turn to stare. A small dog barks at the end of a leash. Nobody moves to help Sam.

Mari turns on Archie. "What the hell?!"

"He was going to hurt you!"

"No he wasn't—you didn't need to hit him. I'm not some damsel in distress here for you to save!"

"You should be thanking me," Archie says, shaking off the pain in his hand.

"And you," Mari says, ignoring Archie and addressing Sam. "My mom has cancer. She might die. Her life might end. And what are you so pissed about? Your girlfriend dumping you? Boo-fucking-hoo. She doesn't want to be with you, and showing up on her doorstep isn't going to change that—we're not in some movie. But you know what? Even though you're a colossally self-absorbed, whiney jackass, you're only eighteen. You will meet other girls. Chances are, some of them are going to be dumb enough to like you. So move on. This isn't the end of your fucking life."

Noticing that Dante is moving to help Sam, Archie turns his anger on him. "Why are you helping that asshole? What—are you in love with him?"

Dante stares at Archie in disbelief, realizing for the first time that his confession was not lost in the storm. But Dante needs to hear someone say it aloud.

"What's that supposed to mean?" Dante finally asks.

A shadow passes over Archie's face. "You know what it means, fag." The word leaves his mouth like an arrow unloosed.

Dante's shoulders sag. His eyes lose their light.

Archie turns around. He puts his hands behind his head and watches the cars rushing by on the highway. He knows it was wrong, but his anger is too fresh to apologize.

Mari shakes her head and walks away from everyone.

Unnoticed, Sam rises to his feet.

He walks back to the car, and he pulls the keys from his pocket.

He opens the driver's side door and climbs behind the wheel.

He starts the car.

Sam peers at his friends through the windshield and sees their faces colored with shock. They're looking at one another, uncertain of what is happening, of what they should—or can—do. As they start to wander toward him, he waves goodbye and pulls out of the parking space. But he only travels a few feet before Archie leaps onto the hood, his body sprawling across the windshield like some gigantic, bespectacled bug.

Sam continues driving but clicks on the windshield wipers. They only swing a few inches before flapping uselessly against Archie's side.

Archie pounds on the windshield with a fist. "Stop the car, dickhead!"

Sam hears Mari and Dante making a similar plea from somewhere nearby. He glances in their direction but cannot see through the plastic bag that now serves as the side window.

Despite the fact that Archie blocks most of his view, Sam accelerates.

Archie clings to the window, holding on with all of his strength. "Are you insane?!" he shouts. "Stop!"

"Sam!" he hears Mari shout. "There's a kid in front of you!"

Sam slams on the breaks. The car skids to a stop. Archie tumbles off the hood and rolls across the pavement. Mari rushes to him.

The window cleared, Sam's eyes scan the area for the child he might have hit.

But there is no kid. Anywhere.

"There's no kid," he says to himself. He slams his fists on the steering wheel. "There's no kid! You lied to me!"

Dante rips open the plastic covering the side window, reaches inside, and plucks the keys from the ignition.

"Get out," he says.

Sam watches as Mari hunches over Archie's crumpled form. People gather around. Some look inside the car at Sam, wondering what the hell is going on. Others take out their phones trying to determine if they should call the police.

Archie stirs and slowly sits up. He shakes his head. He gropes the ground for his glasses. Mari finds them and places them in his palm. He puts them on. One lens is cracked. He flashes everyone a thumbs-up. Mari says something to the small crowd, and they begin to disperse.

Dante repeats his command to Sam. "Get out."

When Sam neither replies nor moves, Dante climbs into the passenger seat.

Sam hangs his head. They sit together in silence.

"Is it true?" Sam asks. "You're gay?"

Dante sighs. And then nods.

"That's cool. Sorry, about last night, though. I can't remember all of what I said. But I'm sure at least some of it was ignorant."

Dante lets the apology hang in the air.

A line of cars begins to accumulate behind them, honking with gathering impatience. Dante hits the hazards, reaches his uninjured arm through the broken window, and gestures for people to drive around.

"I don't know what I did wrong," Sam says.

"You hit Archie with your car."

"No, not that. I mean with Sarah."

"You didn't do anything wrong."

"Then tell me why she dumped me, Dante."

"She moved."

"Bullshit," Sam says. "If she loved me, then she would have at least tried to make this work."

"It's not that simple."

"It is."

"It's not. We always think we know what's going on with other people, but we don't. We can't."

They watch Mari help Archie to his feet. He throws one arm over her shoulder and she helps him limp over to the car. Archie slides into the back seat, and Mari climbs in on the other side. She smacks Sam on the back of the head.

"You could have killed him."

"Sorry," Sam says.

"Why are we still in the middle of the parking lot?" she asks. "Let's go home."

Dante holds up the keys and looks at Sam. "I'm going to put these back in, but don't take off for Seattle. Park, so we can talk this through."

Sam nods. Dante inserts the key and starts the engine, and Sam does as requested.

Everyone gazes out the windows for a long time, watching the cars and people come and go. Nobody speaks because nobody knows what to say anymore. Nothing seems right. Words seem dangerous, as if to speak would be to light a match in room filled with gas.

But Sam eventually does. "I wasn't asleep," he says.

"What are you talking about?" Mari asks.

"Back there. When we pulled over in the storm. I was awake."

"Then why didn't you get out of the car?"

He shrugs. "I just thought, like what's the fucking point? Sarah was the only person who ever cared about me."

All of their minds go to the window that is no more. They had found it busted after they returned to the car once the storm had passed. A mangled, old muffler sat on the front seat amidst the pebbles of broken glass that had not been carried away by the wind.

That was where Sam had been sitting before Dante pulled him out of the car. His head had been leaning against that window.

Dante says, "We care about you."

Sam shakes his head. "It's not the same."

"So does that mean it doesn't matter?" Mari asks.

Sam shrugs.

"Whatever. We do care about you. But we need to go back home, Sam," Mari says. "I need to be with my mom."

Sam says, "There's nothing waiting for me at home."

"There's nothing for you in Seattle, either," Mari says. "And you're not the only one in this car."

"Then I'll go the rest of the way on my own," Sam says. "I'll hitchhike. Like Sunshine."

"No," Archie says, avoiding Dante's eyes, avoiding Mari's. "I think we should keep going. We're nearly there."

Mari turns to Archie in disbelief. "What's the point?"

"I couldn't care less about helping this asshole anymore. But the sooner we go back, the sooner I have to move in with my father."

"And the sooner I have to face my grandparents," Dante adds, avoiding eye contact with Archie or anyone else. "If you couldn't figure it out, I'm in trouble for some reason because I'm gay. I'm not ready to deal with that yet."

"Three against one," Sam points out.

Mari leans back and folds her arms over her chest. "You damn well better pay for that window."

Over Adventure

SUNDAY, 8:19 P.M.

The next thousand miles pass in near silence as Mari, Archie, Sam, and Dante fall into a rhythm.

They drive in three- or four-hour shifts.

They stay in one place only long enough to accomplish necessary tasks. Bathroom. Food. Gas. Repeat.

They pass through the northern plains where the mind-numbing flatness is dotted with grazing cattle. The sparseness is interrupted by small towns consisting of a handful of houses clustered around towering silos. Everything seems to repeat, like the looping background in some old cartoon.

When not driving or sleeping, Mari writes in her notebook, Archie works math problems, Dante contemplates life while watching the landscape slide by, and Sam reads the book Sunshine gave them.

They rarely speak, and when they do, it's only to convey what gestures cannot.

They're over adventure. The destination no longer excites them. It is as if they've brokered a fragile truce to accept the remainder of their trip as mere escape. They're stuck in orbit.

As the sun sets, they approach the mountains of Montana. There's a brief argument about the radio when Sam tries to turn it up while Mari is driving. But Dante quashes the bickering, and the car settles back into its purgatorial silence.

Night falls.

The Slow-Moving World

MONDAY, 3:01 A.M.

Archie brings the car to a complete stop. The glowing red line of taillights stretches so far into the night that he cannot see the source of the backup.

With the plastic over the broken window no longer flapping, radio music rises to the surface. It's some old folk song. Archie listens. He considers changing the station. But he doesn't.

Dante and Sam are asleep in the back, Mari in the front.

After several minutes, there's still no movement ahead. Archie sighs.

He glances at Dante in the rearview mirror.

He sighs again.

Mari stirs. She slowly comes to and takes in the situation. "What's going on?" Her words are thick with sleep. She sits up and stretches. Puts her glasses back on.

"Traffic."

"Looks bad. Know why?"

He shrugs. Leans back.

Mari turns the radio to the AM band and begins scanning for information. Late-night talk radio cuts in and out, rambling about weather or sports or God or politics. Finally, the dial hits a traffic report.

After listening for a few moments they learn of an accident a couple miles up the road. Both westbound lanes are closed.

"I hope everyone's okay," she whispers.

Archie kills the engine and rolls down the window. The soft sounds of idling engines and distant music drift through the air.

"Why'd you say that back there? To Dante?" Mari asks.

Archie considers her question as he gazes into the line of lights. He glances into the rearview mirror and sees cars stacking up behind them. He realizes he's trapped.

"I don't know. It's not like I was planning to say it," Archie says quietly, careful not to wake Dante and Sam.

"But did you mean it?"

Archie shakes his head. "Of course not."

"Then why'd you say it?"

"I don't know, Mari. It just came out. I was upset. I tried to help you, and you yelled at me. I'm sorry. I'm not the best with words."

"I'm not the one you need to apologize to."

Silence settles between them. Archie's mind wanders back to this time last night. He and Mari in the lake. Their arms around each other, bodies pressed together. The silence was good then. It wrapped around them like a soft blanket. Now it has become a wall.

He mourns the difference that twenty-four hours can make.

"That was a horrible thing to say," Mari says. "Dante admitted something to us back there. Something significant. Something he's obviously been holding in for a long time. And that's how you react? With hatred? You're supposed to be his friend."

Archie glances at Dante. His eyes are still closed. "I don't hate Dante."

"If that word—*fag*—could slide out from your lips," Mari says, "that means it must have been living somewhere within you."

Archie looks down at his hands on the steering wheel. "It's not like you said anything when he first told us."

"I didn't have the chance. We were in the middle of a storm, remember?"

"And afterwards?"

"I didn't want to force it. And I didn't know if anybody else heard, so I was waiting for him to bring it up again."

Archie looks out his window and watches a lone car pass in the opposite direction. "I don't hate Dante," he repeats.

"Then what's your problem? I mean, you're not religious, so you're not hung up on that whole homosexuality-as-sin thing, right?"

"No."

"Did someone touch you when you were a kid?"

"Ugh. No."

"Just asking."

Archie fidgets with the wheel. He rubs his clammy palms together. He checks to make sure Dante and Sam are still sleeping. "My parents' divorce . . ." he starts to say but falters.

"What about it?" Mari asks.

He takes a deep breath as if he were about to jump out of a plane. "My parents divorced because my dad came out. As gay."

Mari nods. "So?"

"What do you mean, *so*?"

"So why's that matter? I mean, did he have an affair?"

"I don't think so."

"Did he ever abuse your mom? Ever hit you?"

"No. Never."

"Did he abandon you?"

Archie shakes his head.

"Did you find out he's a serial killer or something?"

"No?"

She takes the glasses off Archie's face, cleans the lenses with her shirt, and then puts them back on. "Then why are you telling me this like you're revealing something terrible about him?"

Mari's question makes Archie feel like he's run off a cliff without realizing there's no ground beneath his feet.

"I don't know," Archie says.

Mari shakes her head. "I thought you were better than this, Arch."

"Sorry that I'm not." He looks at the line of cars, wishing it would start moving again.

"They're gay. So what?" Mari pushes. "I'm black. You're white. We can be together. Why can't he be with whoever he loves?"

Archie turns to Mari. "Are we together?"

"Don't dodge the question."

"It's not that. I'm not logically opposed."

"Then what? It just grosses you out or something?"

"No."

"There has to be a reason, Arch. There's always a reason."

"I don't know what it is, Mari. I'm sorry. I wish I did, but I don't. I can't explain it like I feel it."

"If you care about Dante—if you care about your dad—you need to figure out why the hell you resent who they are. You're hurting them, hurting yourself by rejecting them. I guarantee you'll lose them both if you don't figure this out."

Even as the words leave her mouth, Mari's mind goes to the unopened letter pressed between the pages of her notebook. She tells herself it's a different situation.

Ahead, the collective red glow cast by taillights begins to dim in a chain reaction. Archie turns the key, and the radio comes back to life in the middle of a song. Traffic begins to unclog.

In the shadows of the back seat, Dante's eyes are open. They have been for the last several minutes. He gazes out the window at the slow-moving world.

Pretty Cool People

MONDAY, 6:01 A.M.

After hours of careening through hills and mountains stacked with pine trees, they find themselves on a stretch of road that curves around a corner and delivers them to a small town. Its modest collection of two and three-story brick buildings sit along a handful of streets that lie in a grid on the south side of the highway.

Archie clicks on his turn signal and exits. Sensing the car slowing, Mari, Archie, and Dante awaken.

Archie navigates through the streets, pleased by their mathematical arrangement, looking for somewhere to eat. The first two restaurants he comes across are still closed, but he eventually finds an open diner. He parks along the street and everyone climbs out, yawning and stretching. The air is chilly, but it is fresh so they inhale it greedily. It smells damp and earthy.

A bell jingles as they enter the restaurant, and the fresh air is replaced with a wave of warmth that carries the scents and sounds of breakfast. Coffee brewing. Bacon sizzling. Eggs frying. Toast burning. A few people sitting at the counter turn to them, nod, and then resume their conversations. A skinny guy at the grill behind the counter—who looks like he could pass for twenty or forty—gestures for them to take a seat. He seems to be the only employee.

"Be right with you," he says, his smile revealing a chipped front tooth.

All of the booths in the place are open, so they take the one in the back corner. Sam slides in next to Dante, and Archie sits across from them. Mari heads to the restroom.

Dante pulls out laminated menus from behind the napkin holder and passes them around. They consider their choices in silence.

The chip-toothed cook walks over a moment later bearing a carafe. "Morning, fellas." He smiles, flips the overturned mugs sitting on their paper placemats, and starts pouring. A dragon tattoo snakes around his forearm, its crude lines and colors faded. "Name's Jack."

Dante covers his cup with his hand. "No, thanks."

"It comes with a meal," Jack explains.

"Oh." Dante removes his hand and Jack fills his mug. Steam rises off the coffee, which looks black as ink.

"Creamer and sugar's right there," he says. "I'll give you a minute."

They nod, and he moves away to serve the other customers.

One by one, they decide what they want and set down their menus. Sam scratches the back of his head. Dante grabs a straw and starts twisting it idly. Archie examines the local business ads that decorate the paper placemat.

Mari returns. She looks at the empty seat next to Archie and hesitates before taking it. "So what's everyone getting?" she asks, studying the menu.

"Food," says Sam.

"Oh," Mari says, "I thought you ate shit. You know. Since you're an asshole."

"That doesn't even make sense," Sam says. "Assholes don't eat anything. They expel shit. But maybe we should ask Archie since he's one, too. What do you think, Arch?"

"Ha. Ha."

"We're about to eat," Dante says. "Can we please stop talking about this?"

The conversation lulls, and everyone is relieved when Jack returns a moment later.

He smiles at Mari and then asks, "You ready?" He notices Archie glance at his hands, which are not holding a pad. Jack taps his own forehead. "I got a mind like a bear trap."

They nod and give him their orders.

"Food should be up in about ten," he tells them.

Before he leaves Sam asks, "Hey, how far's Seattle?"

Jack looks out the window as if he can see the city from where he stands. "About five hours. Four and a half if you've got a ride like mine." He nods in the direction of a bright yellow, vintage sports car parked outside.

Jack lingers.

Sensing the guy is accustomed to receiving compliments at this point, Archie obliges. "Nice wheels."

"Thanks." Jack smiles and then wanders back over to the grill.

Sam takes a sip of coffee. It's bitter and burns his tongue.

Dante continues to fidget with the straw.

Mari rests her elbows on the table and stares at nothing.

Archie empties several sugar packets into his mug. He pours in a little cup of creamer, watching the milk swirl and form light brown clouds within the black. There's something comforting in it, some ratio of the spiral that could be deduced with enough effort.

After he finishes stirring his coffee, Archie observes several customers pay their bills and get up to leave, probably off to work. He wonders if they're all headed to the same place. If not, if they're parting ways, maybe they'll meet up afterward for drinks after work. Maybe for them, that's life. And maybe that's enough.

Jack returns a moment later, interrupting Archie's idle thoughts. But he is not carrying any food. He looks from side to side, and then crouches low next to their table. "You guys seem like some really cool people."

"Really?" Archie asks, adjusting his glasses.

Jack lingers as if trying to decide whether or not he wants to say more. "You like animals?" he finally asks.

Archie, Sam, Dante, and Mari look at each other. "Sure," Mari says. "I have a dog. Her name's Macadamia."

Jack slaps the table and then points at Archie. "Killer name. That's what I'm talking about. Look. Here's the deal. I got a bathtub full of baby alligators. Just hatched. Little monsters are cute as hell. You interested?"

"In what?" Mari asks.

Jack smiles and cocks his head. "In taking a few, of course. Keepin' 'em."

"Like as pets or something?" Dante asks.

"Yeah, like pets or something. Train 'em if you want."

"What, exactly, can you train a baby alligator to do?" Archie asks, taking a scientific interest in the possibility.

"How the fuck should I know?" Jack asks.

"Um . . . aren't you the one selling them?" Mari points out.

"Train them to do whatever the hell you want, I guess. Swim laps. Bite on command. Jump through a flaming hoop. It's up to you."

Sam leans forward. "How big are they?"

"Tip to tail, maybe eight or nine inches."

"You know what else is eight or nine inches?" Archie asks the others, testing the waters. Nobody bites. He lets it go. "So how big will they get?"

Jack shrugs.

"Is this even legal?" Mari asks.

Jack tilts a flattened hand from side to side. "Wait—you're not cops are you? If you're cops, you have to tell me."

"Not cops," Archie says.

"Good, good. So what do you say?"

"How much?" Sam asks.

"Fifty each," Jack says, but noticing Sam's reaction, he relents. "Alright, alright. Thirty. Friends and family discount. How many can I put you down for?"

Sam strokes his chin.

"You're not seriously considering this, are you?" Mari asks. "This has to be like animal cruelty."

Jack sighs. "I understand your concern. I am nothing if not a friend to living creatures. I didn't buy the eggs or nothing. They came into my brother's possession in a card game, and he gave 'em to me. So now, I either find the little guys homes or dump them into the sewers."

"That's horrible," Dante says.

"Exactly." Jack taps out a beat on the table and stands. "Let me finish making your breakfast. Think on it. You know where to find me." He winks and returns to the grill.

Mari makes sure Jack is out of earshot and then leans forward. "Should we, like, call the cops on this guy?"

The table falls into silence as they all consider the situation.

But then, like the sun emerging from behind a cloud, Dante starts chuckling. Mari tries to slap his head, but Dante dodges it and flicks his crumpled straw wrapper at her. It catches in Archie's glasses, dangling from the corner of his frames, which causes Mari to break out in laughter. She throws her arm around Archie's neck and shoves a napkin down his shirt, and soon he's chuckling as bad as Dante. She kicks Sam's leg, which triggers a smile. And suddenly even Sam is laughing as he retaliates by tossing an open sugar packet into Mari's hair.

A minor war ensues. Their laughter rises, joining together, as they flick and toss and dodge condiment packages and bits of napkin and straws and crumbs. The other customers turn to watch the strangers, not understanding because how can they? Eventually, they lose interest and turn away.

And just when it seems like it's over, like there's a truce building, Archie catches Mari's eye and they start cracking up all over again. Tears form in their eyes. Their stomachs hurt from laughing so hard at how stupid this is, at how stupid all of this is.

Something shifts. Resentments release. Hearts soften.

Jack returns to their booth and sets their plates in front of them, looking down at the mess they've made. They wipe at their eyes and take deep breaths. Eventually, still smiling, they regain control of themselves.

"Sorry," Mari says. "We'll clean it up."

He nods and then walks away. Their orders having been mixed up, they trade plates.

"Before we start eating," Archie says, "I want to say something." Everyone pauses, their forks hovering above their food. "I want to apologize to you, Dante. I really am sorry for what I said yesterday."

"Thank you, Arch," Dante says. "I appreciate that." Mari reaches across the table and places her hand on his bandaged forearm.

Archie says. "You're my friend, and I hate how I made you feel. I've got some stuff I'm trying to work through, but know that I am trying to figure it out. For you . . . and for my dad."

Sam looks up at Archie, surprised, but Dante just nods. "I know, Arch. I heard you and Mari talking last night."

Archie drops his eyes. "Oh. Sorry."

Dante looks at Archie. "There was nothing you need to apologize for in that."

"So are we cool?"

"Yeah, we're cool." Dante extends his fist and Archie bumps it with his own.

They lower their forks to begin eating, but Sam says, "Wait, guys. I have something to say, too."

Mari looks up. "Oh?"

"Yeah, sorry I've been a flake this past week. And sorry I tried to steal your car, Mari. And sorry, Archie, that I hit you with it."

"It's all right," Archie shrugs. He takes Mari's hand under the table. "I think I understand now how you feel, about wanting to be with someone so bad you'll do anything to be with them."

"Can I eat now, or does someone else have an apology they need to get out?" Dante asks. "My bacon's getting cold."

Nobody says anything, so everyone starts eating.

But then Jack reappears at the end of their booth. "So you in? I'll drop it to twenty each."

"We'll pass," Mari says.

"All right, all right," Jack says. He sighs and runs a hand over his mouth. "Truth is, my girl's real pissed. Likes to take a hot soak in the tub almost every night, ya know? But can't do that seeing as how it's filled with tiny gators. So I just need to get rid of these little fuckers. Heck, you can have as many as you want for free. I make a call, and my girl brings 'em by before you're done with your meal. What do ya say?"

Sam looks at his friends and grins.

What No Longer Matters

Mari wrinkles her nose. "What's that smell?" she asks without taking her eyes off the road.

"Probably Dante," Archie says from the front seat. "Big guy's been ripping farts this whole trip like crazy."

"No, I haven't," Dante says. He reaches forward and flicks Archie's ear.

"No, seriously," Mari says. "It smells like . . . I don't know. But it's nasty."

Dante and Archie sniff, their faces scrunching when they catch the scent.

"Sam?"

Sam sticks his nose into the large bucket and sniffs. "It's definitely not Reptar." He peers at his new friend, the tiny alligator swimming in the shallow water. Its leathery skin speckled with yellow and brown. It looks up at him with its permanent grin and murderous eyes, and begins to claw and scratch the side of the bucket as if trying to escape.

And then out of nowhere, the car stops making its strange sounds, the dying gerbil noise Archie had complained about during his first turn behind the wheel. It is as if the engine has finally cleared its throat.

Mari looks at the others and smiles. "I guess the fresh air's doing the old girl some good."

But then the engine shudders and everything shuts off. The dials on the dashboard all drop to zero. The radio and lights blink off. They feel the car coasting but slowing.

"Shit," she says. She steps on the gas pedal, but nothing happens.

Mari pulls over. "What now?" she asks as the car slows to a stop.

The white wisps are faint at first, and Mari thinks her tired eyes are just playing tricks on her. She tells herself that condensation vapors are slipping out of the vent. But the vapors quickly thicken and darken until they become tendrils of brown smoke.

"Guys?" she asks.

Everyone sits up. The acrid smell becomes overpowering.

"Give it a minute. See if it goes away," Sam says. "Just roll down the windows."

They do. But the smoke thickens and begins to choke the car's interior. Some of it drifts out the open windows, but more smoke pours in. It becomes difficult to see.

Coughing, they grab what they can and pile out.

Cars whiz past, kicking up dust and gravel. The surrounding pine trees rustle in the wind. Sunlight shifts behind the clouds.

Something orange flickers out from beneath the hood.

They step back.

"Um, should we call 911?" Archie asks nobody in particular. Dante takes out his phone.

The flames grow, now undeniable. They hiss and crackle, licking the underside of the hood, trying to escape. A thick, brown smoke billows out of the car and floats into the sky.

"Fuck," says Sam, alligator bucket in one hand, Sunshine's book in the other.

"Yeah," Mari says. "Grab your stuff."

As Dante dials, Sam, Mari, and Archie rush to empty their belongings from the trunk. They swing their bags over their shoulders and scramble down the road ahead of the car, stopping only when they're outside of what Archie deems to be the blast radius.

"They said someone will be here soon," Dante says, sliding his phone back into his pocket.

They set down their things and gaze at the car, watching the fire grow, feeling the heat even from where they stand.

A few minutes pass, and a state trooper pulls up, lights flashing. He steps out of his car, revealing himself to be a small man bearing a small fire extinguisher.

"Y'all back up," he tells them. Carefully, he pops the hood, points the fire extinguisher's hose at the engine, and squeezes the trigger.

But nothing comes out. Not that white, foamy stuff. Not even a puff of air.

Nothing.

"The universe is conspiring against us," Sam says into his bucket.

Dante nods.

"Goddamn cutbacks," the trooper mumbles. He speaks into the radio at his shoulder and then tosses the useless fire extinguisher into the trunk of his patrol car. "Fire department's on its way. But it's local. Volunteer, actually. Probably take a few."

Together, they watch the flames spread, swelling and swirling like something alive until it engulfs the front half of the car. Pieces of the car's frame start to blacken, melt, and sag. They watch the surreal scene, frozen with disbelief.

"Stay over here. I'll be back in a sec to get your info. Call whoever you need to." The trooper disappears into his patrol car and begins tapping away at his computer and talking on his radio.

"My parents are going to kill me." And then Mari realizes her hands are empty. She looks around, digs through her bag, panicked. Not finding what she's looking for, she lifts her eyes to her burning car. "My notebook."

"What about it?" Archie asks.

Her eyes widen as he holds it up. She snatches it away and flips through the pages. She finds something, pulls it out, and presses it to her chest. "Thank you." She wraps her arms around Archie.

"What is that?" he asks, as they pull apart.

"A letter," she says.

"From your other boyfriend?"

"Oh, are you my boyfriend?"

"Don't dodge the question."

"It's from my real mom. My birth mother, I mean."

"I didn't know you had contact with her," Archie says.

"I didn't."

"What's it say?" Dante asks.

Mari turns the thin, unopened envelope in her hands. "I don't know."

"Well we've got time," Archie says, tilting his head toward the conflagration.

There's something about the absurdity of the burning car that makes Mari think of her mom. The cancer lurking within her breast. Waiting to ignite, to consume her mom like the flames devouring the car.

Her mom wanted her to contact her biological mother. It is only now that Mari realizes the simple fact that she has been resisting for selfish reasons. The woman had rejected her, and in her resentment, Mari responded with rejection. She had formed indefensible walls around her heart. And who was that helping in the long run?

She loves her mom so completely and utterly. And if her mom wants Mari to open up those walls, then perhaps she should. And now would be the time to do so.

"I guess you're right," Mari says.

She wanders a few feet away from the others. She takes a deep breath, slides a finger under the flap, and tears the envelope open across the top. After removing the single page and unfolding it, she wonders at the handwriting, so similar to her own. She is surprised to discover that the letter is dated the day she was born.

She reads:

Dearest Marigold,

The first thing you need to know is that I love you. I love you. When I first held you in my hands, it was like when you first notice the flowers blossom in the Spring. That's where your name comes from—my favorite flower. They can grow almost anywhere, and when they do, they're always beautiful.

As I write these words, you're probably in your new home. With your new family. Your new mom and dad are probably holding you tightly to their chests, to their hearts, as I did just an hour ago. Falling in love with you.

They're good people. I chose them over all the others. There was something I sensed that told me to trust that they would give you all the love you need, all the love you deserve.

All the love that I can't give you right now.

But this letter isn't about why that is. There are some things that just can't be explained in writing. I hope that when you're ready, we can get to know each other. I hope we talk, and I can explain everything then. And I pray you'll understand.

No, this letter is about the simple fact of how much I love you. How this is the hardest thing I've ever done, the hardest thing I'll ever do.

I will think of you every day. I've asked your new mom to keep me updated on your life, and I will wait for the day you're ready to contact me like withered plants wait for rain.

And as you read these words, know that I will be waiting for you.

Love always,
Your first mother

Mari refolds the letter and tucks it back into the envelope. Then, she starts to cry.

Nobody asks what the letter says, because they all sense the question would be sacrilegious. They sense she needs to grieve, needs to process alone. But they also sense she needs to know she is not alone. So they join her. Archie hugs her, Dante puts a hand on her shoulder, and even Sam inches a bit closer to the group.

Mari exhales and wipes her eyes with the cuff of her hoodie.

"You still want Sam to replace that window?" Archie asks.

Mari laughs through her tears. "My parents are going to be pissed. And how are we going to get you to Seattle now, Sam?"

Sam gazes as the burning car. "It really does seem like every force in the universe is trying to tell me not to go. Maybe it's time I listen."

But Mari shakes her head. "My car's not giving her life for nothing. We can't control the world, but we can control how we react to it. We'll find a way."

The short trooper walks over, interrupting their moment. "My guess? Electrical fire. I could be wrong. Either way, you're not going to be able to drive this thing anymore." He gestures to Mari's still burning car as if that were even a possibility. "You'll probably want to call a tow truck to take it to the nearest junkyard."

Mari sighs.

The trooper adjusts his sunglasses. "You got someone who can pick you up? Based on those Jersey plates, I assume you're a long way from home."

Sam, Mari, Dante, and Archie look at one another.

The trooper rubs the back of his neck. "Well, maybe the tow truck can take—" he stops speaking as his eyes land on the book in Sam's hand, the copy of *On the Road* that Sunshine gave them. "That what I think it is?"

Sam tilt's the cover toward him. "A book?"

The trooper laughs. "Mind if I have a look?"

Sam hands it over. The trooper takes it, and turns it over, handling it carefully like a relic. He runs his hand over the cover, opens it to the copyright page, and scans the tiny print.

"Well I'll be a monkey's uncle. First edition." His eyes flick between them and the book. "I majored in English in college until I read this book."

"And then what?" Archie asks.

"I dropped out of school and traveled the country."

"And now you're a police officer," Sam observes.

"I'll tell you what," the trooper says, rubbing his chin. "You let me have this, and I'll give you a ride to wherever you were headed."

Mari looks at Sam and smiles. She turns back to the trooper. "Seattle," she says.

"Great!" The trooper says. "Just sit tight a moment." He returns to his car.

"You actually seem to be taking this all pretty well," Archie says to Mari. He takes her hand and squeezes it.

She smiles at him. She looks at Sam and Dante standing next to her. She feels the letter in her other hand, its paper weight insubstantial. She watches her car burn.

"It's just a car. We have to let go of what no longer matters."

Three Thousand Miles

MONDAY, 2:48 P.M.

After the firefighters extinguished the flames.

And the paramedics checked vision and breathing and pulse.

And they called home.

After the yelling and the apologies and the relief.

After hotel arrangements were made for the night and plane tickets purchased.

The state trooper dropped them off in front of Sarah's school.

He would have preferred to leave them at someone's house, but that was all they had. None of them had Sarah's new address yet, not even Sam, and she wasn't answering their texts and calls. And, of course, he had made a deal.

So it is; they now sit on a bench in front of the school with all their smoke-scented belongings, watching the doors and waiting.

"So they started last week?" Archie asks.

"Yup. This should be Sarah's first day, though." Sam checks his watch. "Ten minutes."

He leans back. And then forward. He lifts the shirt draped over the bucket and checks on Reptar. He replaces the cover. He glances at his watch again.

"What are you going to say?" Archie asks.

Sam shakes his head. He pulls out a cigarette. He fidgets with his lighter, flicking the flint wheel over and over again, just enough to make it spark. But he does not light it.

Dante watches the clouds. Archie and Mari hold hands and whisper to one another.

Kids start to trickle out of the building even though the bell has not yet rung. Some glance at Sam and the others, casting them a confused look as they continue on their way.

Finally, the bell rings. A moment later, the doors burst open and teenagers spew forth. They rush out of the building in a loud, chattering mass. Many run off, but several linger in clumps, waiting for rides or just hanging out.

Sam stands up on the bench and scans the sea of faces. "Help me look for her."

His friends raise their eyes in search of Sarah.

But after a few minutes, the flow begins to lighten and there is still no sign of their erstwhile rogue.

"Maybe there's another exit," Dante says. "I'll check the back."

"Good idea," Sam says, eyes glued to the crowd.

Dante walks away and disappears around the side of the building.

"Maybe she was out sick today," Mari offers, but Sam ignores her.

As the minutes pass, the clumps drift away and the crowd thins out. Fewer and fewer students emerge from the building, like water trickling from a tap being slowly turned off.

Dante returns. "She's not over there." But he grins, and holds up a scrap of paper. "I did get a number, though."

"You dog," Mari says, nudging him with her elbow. "You actually hit on someone?"

"I didn't even do anything," Dante explains, blushing as he tucks the paper into his pocket. "These two guys just walked up and started talking to me. They were really nice. When I told him I needed to get back to you guys, one of them slipped me this and said we should hang out sometime."

"You going to call him?" Mari asks. "We have the rest of the day."

"Nah. But it just feels good having it."

Archie says, "Good for you, D."

And then. Suddenly. Like a firefly glowing in the darkness. Sarah appears.

Sam instantly recognizes her, even though she has already cut her hair and dyed it a purplish red. Even though her eyes are darkened with mascara. Even though she's walking with unfamiliar friends.

"There she is," Mari points, although Sam has already seen her.

But Sam, still standing on the bench, does not move.

He does not call out.

He watches as she and her friends stop on the sidewalk. They gather in a circle and start talking. She swings her bangs out of her eyes and then laughs at something someone says. It is a laugh Sam knows. A laugh he misses. A laugh that cuts him somewhere deep inside.

Sarah does not notice her old friends.

Sam puts the unlit cigarette between his lips.

"You want me to go over?" Archie asks, moving to stand.

But Sam does not respond. He does not move as he continues gazing at Sarah.

She readjusts the bag slung over her shoulder and laughs again, this time covering her mouth.

The gesture triggers a memory in Sam's mind. Halloween. Freshman year.

Sarah had gone to a party while Sam stayed in to watch a classic monster movie marathon on television. She had eventually called him from the party, horribly drunk, wanting a ride home.

He took his dad's car, even though he didn't have his license yet, and drove to the party. A visibly smashed Sarah—decked out as a zombie princess—spilled into the passenger seat. Three other people slid into the back. They were in costume, so Sam didn't know who they were—but probably wouldn't have recognized them even if they had not been in disguise.

"Samwise!" Sarah said, slurring the word. She had leaned over and kissed the side of his mouth, sloppy and reeking of cheap beer. "I told Amy, Hannah, and Heather you could take them home. Hope that's cool."

"Sure," Sam had said.

"Radical. I told you he's the best boyfriend ever!"

And so Sam drove as they talked too loudly about what they drank, how much they drank, and how drinking made them feel. The relief he felt when the last one stepped out of the car was immeasurable. And then Sarah leaned into him and slid her hand over his crotch. "Let's go to your place," she had whispered into his ear.

Thinking he might at least get something out of his good deed, he agreed. She made way too much noise as they snuck down to his room, but nobody woke up to investigate. As soon as they made it to the basement, Sarah began peeling off Sam's clothes between kisses. Her motions were awkward and sloppy, leaving no doubt in Sam's mind that she had had too much to drink.

Still. Sam was a boy. He had dropped what he was doing to be his girlfriend's designated driver. He had been a good boyfriend. Didn't he deserve this?

Sarah pulled off her tattered zombie princess gown. Giggling, she fell back onto his bed in her bra and panties, face still made up like the undead. Eyes at once wild and unfocused. She beckoned to him.

But Sam stayed where he was.

"I'm kind of tired," Sam said. "I'm just going to sleep on the couch upstairs."

But Sarah sat up and, unsteadily, grabbed his wrists and tried pulling him on top of her. But he resisted. "What's wrong,

Samwise? Is it the makeup? If it's the makeup, I can clean it off first, if you want."

"It's not that," he said. "I really am just tired."

And then Sarah went quiet. She stopped pulling on him. Stopped swaying. Suddenly, her stomach heaved and her hand shot up to cover her mouth. But it was too late. Her cheeks puffed up. Vomit pushed through, leaking from between her fingers, trickling onto her bare thighs, splattering onto Sam's bed.

She rushed away, up the stairs. Sam followed after her.

He had spent the rest of the night in the bathroom with Sarah, holding her hair back as she alternated between sobbing and throwing up, apologizing and promising to never drink again.

And Sam suddenly understands. It took three thousand miles, but he finally gets it: *He* had been a good boyfriend, but *she* had been a shitty girlfriend.

"Earth to Sam," Mari says, interrupting Sam's memory. "They're getting away. What's the plan?"

Sam looks up and watches as Sarah and her group of new friends start walking away.

Sam hops down from the bench. He takes the unlit cigarette from his mouth and tosses it into a nearby garbage can. "Fuck it. Let somebody else hold her hair back."

They turn to him. "Huh?" Archie asks.

Sam says, "Let's go."

"Are you serious?" Dante asks.

Sam nods.

Mari shakes her head. "After all we've been through? Three days in the car. All of our fighting. A tornado. My car burning to ash. And now—"

"Sorry to drag you all this way for nothing."

"Meh," Archie says. "Some things you just can't see at home."

"So now what?" Dante asks.

"The day is ours," Mari says.

Sam says, "I still have my dad's credit card. Let's see the sights. Isn't there, like, some spaceship downtown?"

"The Space Needle," Archie corrects. He takes out his phone. "I'll call a cab."

And then.

Sam picks up Reptar and walks away.

In the Rearview Mirror

MONDAY, 11:48 P.M.

The television glows through the darkness playing some sci-fi movie from the nineties. Mari and Archie are asleep in one bed, and Sam is snoring on a cot.

On the second bed, Dante lies awake staring absently at the screen. Whenever a car passes, his eyes follow the light cast by its headlights as it sweeps across the walls.

He thinks about the day.

The cab had dropped them off at Pike Place Market. They had found some stairs to a lower level and wandered through the maze of small stores without buying anything. From there they walked to the aquarium, where Mari forced Sam to hand over Reptar. They let Sam grieve as they strolled through the angular paths of Olympic Sculpture Park and spent an inordinate amount of time puzzling over some gigantic red steel sculpture that was supposedly an eagle. Then they made their way to the Space Needle and rode the elevator to the observation deck just in time to watch the sun set over the flat waters of Puget Sound.

Afterward, they had bought ice cream and ate it on the curb while joking about skipping out on their flight home the next day to hike Mount Rainier. They talked about what all had happened in the past week and a half and what might happen next year. They mourned Archie's transferring schools. They debated who would be grounded for the longest.

But it is not any of this that's keeping Dante awake right now.

A crumpled piece of paper with a phone number scrawled in pencil. That is what's keeping Dante awake.

And that is why Dante slips out of bed, pulls the paper from the pocket of his jeans, and steps out of the room. Outside now, he walks past the row of closed doors to the vending machines. He leans against one of them and lets its electric hum vibrate through his body. He slips his phone from his pocket.

As he stares at the numbers, his heart begins to race, his hands begins to tremble.

He wishes his phone could text. But since it can't, he takes a deep breath and dials.

It rings a few times, but just when he's about to end the call, someone answers.

"Yeah?" says a slurred voice. "What's up?"

"Um . . . it's Dante . . ."

". . . Who?"

"We met outside the school today? You gave me your number?"

There's some rustling at the other end. Sounds like people talking in the background. The voice returns. "Yeah, yeah . . . Dante . . . What's up, man?"

"Sorry—too late?"

More rustling. "No, no, it's all good." Laughter in the background. Probably the television. "So you want to talk, or what?"

"Or what. Let's meet," Dante says.

"Now?"

"If you can."

It sounds like the guy covers the phone as he talks to someone who is with him. More laughter. Eventually, he says, "Sure, why the hell not. Where are you?"

Dante tells him the name of the motel.

"All right, be there in a few."

Dante lowers himself to the concrete, his back against the vend-ing machine and legs splayed out in front. He listens to the world buzz: the vending machines, the fluorescent lights, the motel's sign, the insects. A car whooshes past. The cackle of a laugh track rises through the open window of a nearby room.

Dante lets his eyelids droop . . .

He does not know how long he's been asleep when he wakes to a pair of headlights shining into his eyes. He shields the glare with his bandaged arm and climbs to his feet.

Dante squints into the light. At first he figures it's the guy, but there seems to be two shapes moving within the car, a black SUV.

The driver side window slides down. A head pokes out. "Dante?"

"Yeah, it's me," Dante smiles, relieved.

He walks out of the headlight beams and up to the window. He glances at the passenger seat. It's empty. He must be so tired he's seeing things.

The guy smiles at Dante. "So."

Dante shifts his weight from one foot to the other. He puts his hands in his pockets. "So."

The guy looks around, checking out the motel. "Spared no expense, eh?" He tilts his head toward the passenger side door. "Get in."

Dante looks around, though he's not sure what he's looking for. His grandparents, maybe. His pastor. Jesus on the Cross.

But then he thinks of his coworker Marco and his beach house fantasy. Sam and Mari in the lake. Zaius and his friends around the fire. If they can all be happy, why can't he?

He remembers Zaius's words: *You're travelers. So travel.*

Given the trouble he'll be in when they return home, Dante figures it will be a long time before he gets another chance.

So he climbs into the front seat. The radio is playing, but the volume is set so low it's barely audible. The car's interior reeks of cheap body spray and alcohol. He buckles up and nods, wondering if this was a mistake.

The guy winks, kicks the car into gear, and drives around to the back of the motel. He pulls into a shadowy corner of the lot, next to the dumpster. He throws the car into park. He kills the engine. "So," he says. His eyes slide over Dante's body.

Dante's heart thuds against his rib cage. He feels heat rise to his face. "So."

The guy leans back and starts undoing his belt. "Mind your teeth."

Dante forces a laugh.

The guy pauses. He smirks. "Oh, you want me to suck you off first?"

Dante reaches for the door handle. This is not what he was looking for. This is not what Zaius and Lamont have, not what Mari and Archie have found, not what Sam and Sarah lost.

"Maybe I should—"

The guy presses a button and the doors lock with a swift whir and click. He presses another button. The child safety locks, Dante realizes.

"Don't tell me you had me drive all the way out here—in the middle of the night—for nothing," the guy says. He runs a hand over this mouth and exhales. "You're down with this, right?"

"Huh?" Dante tries to pull the lock up, but it won't budge.

"I mean you *are* gay, right?"

"Yeah, but—"

"Told you he was a fag," a voice says from behind.

But before Dante can turn to see who spoke, a plastic bag slips over his head. It tightens around his neck, digging into his throat. His world becomes a blur.

He tries to cry out but can't.

He gasps for air and sucks in a mouthful of plastic.

His hands fly up to his neck.

As his fingers scramble for purchase to rip the bag away, something slams into his side and pain radiates along his ribs. He tries to ignore it, to focus on tearing off the bag, but he is struck again and again. The blows keep falling. He feels something in his chest snap and a fire spread along his side.

Something slams into his face and his pain blossoms within his cheek.

He swings out blindly, trying to break the window, block the punches, do some damage of his own.

His fist connects with something hard, and he hears one of his attackers cry out.

Dante thrashes and kicks even harder.

But the bag tightens even more around his neck, cutting off his windpipe.

He is hit over and over again in his ribs, his head, his face.

Jolts of pain. Flashes of red.

Black spots form behind his eyes.

Snot or blood or tears run down his face.

His throat burns.

His head feels both heavy and light.

With each raspy attempt to suck in air, the plastic wrinkles, catching deeper in his nostrils and mouth.

He hears laughter, but it sounds miles away. It's "smear the queer" all over again. He never escaped.

Overcome by a wave of exhaustion, he thinks that maybe this is for the best.

He stops kicking. He stops thrashing.

Like a stretch of midnight road in the rearview mirror, he fades away.

Can't Take a Joke

TUESDAY, 1:12 A.M.

Ever since he heard the heavy door clicked closed, Archie hasn't been able to fall back to sleep.

At first, he did not mind. It was nice.

Lying with Mari. His arm around her. Her head resting on his chest. The credits of some movie scrolling on the TV in the darkness.

He hadn't been able to stop smiling as he thought of the last few days and imagined what the future held for them.

But now something's bugging him. A dark feeling hovering just out of reach.

He knows it was Dante who stepped out because his giant form is missing from his bed. And he knows Dante is alone because Sam's still snoring away.

But Archie has no idea how long he's been gone.

He waits for Dante to return.

He feels the need to pee, so he unravels himself from Mari and makes his way to the bathroom. He urinates, but he does not flush.

He starts to climb back into bed and then hesitates. Changing his mind, he slips on his glasses and heads out the door.

Sam looks around. With Dante nowhere in sight, he randomly selects a direction and starts walking. The cement sidewalk is cold against his bare feet. As he passes the other rooms, he wonders how many people are having sex at that very moment.

He shakes off the distraction and tries to put himself in Dante's shoes, tries to understand why the big guy might sneak away in the middle of the night. Arriving at an answer, he turns around and heads for the vending machines.

But Dante is not there.

He starts to really worry.

He heads back to the room.

"Dante's gone," he announces, flipping on the lights as the heavy door slams closed behind him.

Sam covers his head with a pillow. Mari shifts and reaches for her glasses.

"What?" she asks. "What's going on? What time is it?"

Archie checks the bathroom but it's still empty. "Dante's missing."

"I'm sure he just stepped out for a moment."

"I walked around outside—there's no sign of him anywhere," Archie says, pacing.

"Did you try the vending machines?" Sam asks from beneath his pillow.

"Try his phone," Mari suggests.

Archie grabs his cell and dials Dante. It rings several times and then goes to voicemail. He shoots Mari a pleading look.

Mari rises from the bed and slips on her shoes. "Let's look outside again."

She pokes Sam. He withdraws into the comforter like a hermit crab disappearing into its shell. "He's a big boy. He can take care of himself. Good night."

"Come on, Sam," Mari says. "He's your friend."

When Sam still does not move, Mari and Archie give up on him and head outside.

The building is L-shaped with rooms on either side running along two floors. Their room is in the middle of the first floor, facing the road.

Mari points in one direction. "I'll walk this way." She points in the other. "Go that way. We'll meet around back."

Archie nods and takes off in his assigned direction.

The hallway's clear, so Archie surveys the lot as he walks. Not a person in sight. Just a single row of parked cars, windshields reflecting the neon glow of the motel's sign. One of the letters flickers. The road is empty. The evening is quiet except for the buzzing of the motel's lights.

As Archie turns the corner, he starts to wonder if this is his fault. Did Dante leave because of what he said? He apologized back in the diner, and Dante seemed to accept it. But what if he really didn't? He had hid his homosexuality from them for years, so who's to say he could not hide a grudge?

Archie hears something, interrupting his guilty thoughts. Muffled sounds. Dull thuds.

Archie turns toward the noises. They seem to be coming from near the dumpsters. But it's difficult to see. The light from the motel's sign is blocked by the corner of the building, obscuring the area in shadows.

Creeping closer, he makes out a black SUV parked next to the dumpster. It's rocking back and forth.

Archie asks himself if it's possible. Is that Dante in there? *With* someone?

He sneaks closer. There's a flurry of movement behind the tinted windows. Again, Archie can't see through the darkness— and he's not sure he wants to.

If it is Dante, good for him, right? Archie's not supposed to care about who his friend loves, but neither does he have to watch. Archie's muscles relax. He starts back for the room.

But then he hears a shout—a shout of pain, not pleasure.

He turns back toward the SUV. Sneaking behind the dumpster, he peeks around the side of it into the vehicle's interior, now only a few feet away.

His stomach drops. His mouth goes dry. His muscles lock.

This can't be real.

Through the windshield, he sees someone who he's pretty sure is Dante. Only there's a plastic bag smothering his face. A guy sitting in the back seems to be holding the bag over Dante's head, while a guy behind the wheel keeps punching Dante over and over again.

It can't be real. Who in the hell does something like this?

Archie's first instinct is to shout for help. But the cry catches in his throat. He tries to leap from behind the dumpster, but it's like his feet are glued to the cement. He finds himself frozen with fear, with indecision.

He watches as Dante stops struggling. There's something unnatural in the way his limbs suddenly go limp. Something unnerving in the attackers' laughter.

Forcing himself to move, Archie glances around for something he can use as a weapon. He spots a pothole nearby, its edges ringed with loose pieces of pavement. He runs over and grabs a heavy chunk the size of a football. He hefts it over his shoulder, takes a couple steps, and lobs it into the air.

The chunk of cement hits the windshield and the glass bursts. It does not shatter completely, but instead sags under the weight of the rock, a web of cracks radiating outward.

The guy behind the wheel looks up and spots Archie. He says something Archie cannot hear. The guy in the backseat releases the bag. The rear door, behind Dante, opens.

Archie rushes at the guy as he emerges, throwing a wild punch. The guy easily dodges it and then grips Archie by the collar. He slams Archie into the side of the SUV and buries a fist into his stomach. The air rushes from Archie's lungs. He crumples to the ground.

The guy spits on him. "Fucking faggots." He rears his leg back to deliver a kick to Archie's head.

"Stop!"

The guy actually stops and turns to look just as Sam dives at him. In some poor attempt at a tackle, Sam wraps his arms around the guy's legs.

"The fuck is this?" The guy twists away, freeing himself from Sam's awkward, feeble grip. "How many of you fuckers are there?"

The other guy starts to climb out from behind the wheel to join the fight, but Mari slams his door shut.

"Four," she says. Holding her phone to her ear with her other hand, she adds, "A few more might be joining us. They'll probably bring handcuffs."

"Forget them. Let's get out of here," the driver calls to his friend. And then to Mari. "God. We were just fucking with him. Can't you take a joke?"

The other guy yanks open the front door on the passenger's side. He pulls out Dante, letting his body collapse onto the pavement, and then takes his place in the front seat. The SUV reverses and then peels out of the parking lot, tires squealing.

As Mari explains what is happening to the 911 dispatcher, Archie rushes over to Dante's side. He yanks the plastic bag off Dante's head and rolls him onto his back.

"Dante?" Archie asks, laying his hands on his large friend. Sam peers over his shoulder.

Dante's face is bruised and bloody. His eyes are closed, his lips blue. He is motionless.

"No, no, no," Archie says. He does not know what to do.

Sam says, "Check his pulse."

Archie presses his fingers to the side of Dante's neck. He tries to calm himself enough so he can feel for a heartbeat.

But there's nothing.

Inventing Constellations

TUESDAY, 1:26 A.M.

"Dante. Please, Dante," Archie cries over the body of his friend. "I'm sorry."

"You know CPR?" Mari asks.

Archie does. He took a class once. He regains his composure, tries to remember everything. He sits up. Sets his hands over the center of Dante's chest. He starts pressing down in time with "Row, Row, Row Your Boat" just like he was taught. He counts to thirty. Stops. Pinching the bridge of Dante's nose, Archie tilts his friend's head back and blows into his mouth.

Dante's massive chest rises.

And then falls.

It does not rise again.

Archie looks up at Mari, lost.

"Do it again," she says.

Archie repeats. Presses his chest thirty times. Gives Dante his breath.

Watches his chest rise . . . and fall . . .

Dante sputters and coughs.

Archie smiles, leans back. He looks from Sam to Mari and then back to Dante. "It's me. It's us. We're here. You're safe now. You okay, buddy?"

Dante coughs a few more times. His eyes flutter open. Blood-shot. Unfocused. "Am I dead?" His voice is faint and hoarse.

Archie laughs. "No, big guy. I cast a resurrection spell."

"Help me up," Dante says.

"Maybe you should—"

But Dante is already pushing himself up. His movements are slow and stiff, so Sam and Archie help him into a sitting position on a curb.

"We should get you to the hospital," Archie says.

Dante breathes in and out slowly, testing his lungs. He touches his hands to his mouth, it comes away bloody. He spits. A sharp pain burns in his side. Probably a broken rib or two. "No—I'm all right. Let's just go back to the room."

"We have to wait for the police," Mari says, still on the line. "By the way, anyone happen to get the plate number on that SUV?"

"Of course," Archie says and rattles off the numbers and letters from memory.

Down the hallway, the ice machine rumbles. A door opens and then closes.

"You sure you don't want to go to the hospital?" Sam asks.

Dante rubs his throat and nods.

"So you want to tell us what happened?" Archie asks.

Dante shrugs. "I'm gay. Some people don't seem to like that."

Dante's words hang in the air. Archie looks down at his feet.

"I'm not like them," Archie finally says.

"But you don't like it, do you? That I'm gay."

"It's not that."

"Then what?"

"This. Look at you. Look at what they did to you."

Dante nods.

Archie starts to say something else, but an old woman in a bathrobe suddenly appears from around the corner. She stops short upon seeing the three boys sitting there, one of them beaten bloody.

"Jesus H. Christ! You boys been fighting?" She's holding a bucket in one hand and a half-empty bottle of Jack Daniel's with her other.

"Something like that," Dante says.

She looks at Archie and Sam, puzzled that they appear uninjured, then turns to Dante.

"Here. Looks like you need it more than I do." He shakes his head. "Let me fetch you some ice, then. Just sit tight." The old woman trots away.

They wait for her in silence. They hear the ice machine rumble, and a few moments later the woman reappears. She hands the bucket to Dante. "Here, take this." She hands him a towel that had been draped over her shoulder.

"Thanks," Dante says. "Thank you."

The woman nods and then returns to her room.

"Here." Archie takes the towel from Dante and spreads it out on the ground. He pours some ice onto it and then ties it up. He hands it back to Dante.

Dante presses it against his side. "Thanks."

"I just don't understand," Archie says, crossing his arms.

"What?"

"Why didn't you just wait?"

"For what?"

"To, you know . . . come out."

"Why should I have waited?"

"People can be pretty horrible."

"So what, Arch?"

Archie looks down at his feet. "Why not wait? Until you're somewhere safe where nobody is going to do something like this to you."

"Like where?"

"Geez, I don't know. San Francisco."

Dante laughs, wincing as it triggers pain. "Don't you think I've thought about that, Arch? Don't you think I haven't thought about waiting until college to come out? Or don't you think I've thought about never telling anyone at all?"

"So why did you?"

"I realized it's never going to be safe, Arch. Nowhere is, for anyone. Not for people like me and your dad." Archie bristles at the mention of his father, but Dante continues. "Not even for you. Or Mari. Or Sam. Horrible people are everywhere."

Archie scratches the back of his head and kicks idly at some loose pieces of gravel. Sam listens to their conversation, trying to understand.

Dante continues. "But you get to a point, Arch, where you just get sick of hiding, of lying to everyone. You have to stop caring what they think to survive. Because that feeling—that silencing you're doing to yourself—it becomes worse than anything anyone else could ever do to you."

"Even this?" Archie gestures toward the bruises on Dante's beaten body.

Dante nods. "Even this."

"You sure?"

"Constantly living with that fear? That shame? It's a million times worse than this."

"I don't know if I agree with that. It scares the hell out of me that something like that could happen to you . . . or to my dad."

"But most people aren't horrible," Dante says.

"I beg to differ," Sam says. Archie nods.

"What about that woman who gave me the ice? Zaius and the others? Sunshine? Mari? You guys? You're still here."

"Don't think I've been much help," Sam says. "Being all obsessed with Sarah, I kind of forgot anyone else existed."

Archie says, "And I clearly haven't been what you needed me to be. The friend you've needed."

"Then start now. And when we get home, be the son your father needs."

"I'll try."

"Good," Dante says, readjusting the bundle of ice.

Sam nods.

"They're on their way," Mari says as she returns, sliding her phone back into her pocket. She wipes her eyes. Seeing her boys sitting on the curb, all sad-looking, she kisses them each on the top of the head and then sits down next to Archie.

They lift their eyes to the stars. It is a clear night, the kind of night for inventing constellations.

A letter starts to flicker in the motel's sign. But just as it looks like it's about to blink out, the light returns, glowing brighter and steadier than before.

"Can I ask you something?" asks Archie.

"Sure," Dante answers.

"And promise you'll answer honestly?"

"Of course."

"You ever think about *me* . . . you know . . . sexually?"

They all laugh.

"No offense, Arch," Dante chuckles. "But you're not my type."

Archie shakes his head. "Story of my life."

Mari leans her head against Archie's shoulder and takes his hand. "Not anymore."

Broken and Healed, Awake

TUESDAY, 6:52 A.M.

Archie, Sam, Mari, and Dante gaze at the tarmac through their reflections in the window. Workers in bright orange vests and huge headsets bustle about the plane in the dawn's grey light. They attach a fuel line. They empty the cargo hold of bags, and they load it with new ones. They inspect the body of the aircraft to ensure it's safe for flight. In the distance another plane rolls down the runway and rises into the sky.

There is an announcement. Their flight has been delayed three hours. Storms in the Midwest. The friends set down their bags and sit on the floor in a circle.

"What are we going to do for three hours?" Sam asks.

"I've got an idea," Mari says. She reaches into her bag and brings out a folder. From the folder, she pulls out a square of paper that she unfolds and lays out in the middle of their circle.

They all smile. It's their Dungeons & Dragons game map.

But then Dante points out, "We don't have any dice. Or our figures."

Archie holds up his phone. "Dice app! And we can just use scraps of paper for our characters."

"And we're still out a rogue," Dante adds.

"I think we'll manage," Sam says.

Dante shrugs. "So where were we?"

Mari smiles. She hands out the rest of the character sheets and sets up the folder like a shield. She pulls out her notebook and turns to the page filled with their adventure.

She reads, "You walk into the village and find it completely destroyed. Everywhere you look the ruins of huts and buildings are still smoldering. Charred corpses litter the ground as far as the eye can see—including that of your unfortunate rogue, Leera." She winks at Sam. He laughs. She continues, "A handful of survivors forlornly pick through the rubble, perhaps looking for their valuables . . . or the bodies of their loved ones. You see a maiden—"

"Is she hot?" Archie interrupts.

"What?" Mari said.

"You know, is she hot? What's she look like?"

Mari glares at Archie.

Sam grins.

Dante starts chuckling in short bursts of deep laughter that sound like an engine trying to catch.

Archie removes his glasses, breathes onto the lenses, and then wipes them with the bottom of his shirt. "Well?"

"She's average. An average maiden."

"Average can be hot. Seriously. What's she look like?"

"What's it matter?" Mari says. "She's fictional. Just a random peasant in the background."

Archie shrugs. "So? I want to feel like I'm there. Paint me a picture."

Dante's laughter rises. Sam's smile widens.

Mari sighs. "She looks . . . *average*. She wears *average* clothes. She is of *average* height. She has an *average* build."

Archie considers this. "An average build, you say . . . so that would be like a B-cup? Or C?" He cups his hands in front of his own chest and grins. He moves them outward and awaits confirmation from Mari. Mari says nothing, so Archie continues to expand his imaginary bosom to pornographic proportions.

Mari scratches something out in her notebook and then resumes the story. "The maiden trips over a stone and dies."

"Oh, my," Archie says. "Poor girl."

They continue.

As it usually does, it comes down to the boss battle. This time, the boss is an evil, winged minotaur that calls itself Sh'rgoth. This is the creature that has been terrorizing the countryside for so many years.

They have been battling Sh'rgoth for almost an hour straight. He is close to death, but only Mari knows exactly how close. The others fight on, waiting and hoping for its death, doing what they can to prevent their own.

Which is proving difficult. Archie's mage has used up his best spells. Sam's cleric has been rendered paralyzed. Dante's warrior is poisoned and on the brink of death.

It is Sh'rgoth's turn to attack. He swings his flaming broad sword in a sweeping arc that affects all members of the party. They roll for damage using the app on Archie's phone.

Archie takes five.

Sam takes seven.

Luckily, Dante only takes one.

It's not a lot of damage, but it's enough that Dante knows he will probably not survive another turn. This one has to count.

There is an announcement. Their plane has arrived. Preboarding will begin shortly. But the four friends stay on the floor, stay in their world.

It is Sam's turn, but he is paralyzed so gets skipped.

"What do you want to do?" Mari asks Dante.

"I strike." Dante's finger hovers above Archie's phone. It is much less climactic than rolling an actual die, but such is life.

He taps the screen.

Everyone leans in to watch the digital twenty-sided die spin in place.

"Twenty!" Dante shouts, as the animation stops. He raises his hands in victory. "Critical hit!"

But before they celebrate too much, they turn to Mari, who is calculating Dante's attack roll against the demon's defenses in her notebook behind the folder-screen.

She puts her pen down. Lifts her eyes to the party. Adjusts her glasses.

She says, "Sh'rgoth lets out an agonizing cry as the great axe sinks into his chest. His wings go limp, and he falls from the sky. His massive body, so strong and feared for centuries, slams into the ground below. The heroes rejoice over the crumpled form of their defeated foe."

Sam and Dante and Archie celebrate with cheers and high-fives and hugs. Mari joins them. People stare, but the friends couldn't care less.

"Well played, guys," she says.

"That was a great quest, Mari," says Dante.

"Brilliant," Archie says.

"Can't wait until next week," adds Sam.

All around them, people stand and gather their things. The first boarding announcement crackles over the speaker. An imperfect line forms. Archie, Mari, Sam, and Dante hurry up and put everything from their game back into the folder.

They finish just as their section is called. They stand, still in a daze from the game.

Archie looks around the airport. He considers the destination board with its projected time of departure and arrival. He casts one more glance at the plane that will carry them over and across the continent.

"This isn't travelling," he says.

The others nod. Without speaking, their minds fill with everything they've been through by themselves in the last few weeks, and then everything they've been through together in the last few days. Sneaking away in the middle of the night. Picking up a hitchhiker. Swimming naked in a lake. Surviving a tornado. Fighting with each other. Obtaining a free baby alligator. Watching the car burn. Going to Seattle for no reason and every reason. Saving Dante. Saving each other.

They step forward. Real life awaits. Together, they prepare to board, nervous and brave, broken and healed, awake and ready to return.